SOMETHING ABOUT RUTH

JC MILLER

CONTENTS

Dedicated to mothers

JC Miller/ Something About Ruth

ISBN: 978-1-7339386-8-6 (paperback)

ISBN: 978-1-7339386-9-3 (hardback)

Library of Congress Control Number: 2023900004

This is a work of fiction. Any references to historical events, real people, or real places are used fictitiously. Names, characters, and places are products of the author's imagination or used in a fictitious manner.

Book graphic design: Chanel Smith, WPD Media LLC

Editing: Tee Marshall, Marshall Editing and Consulting

Printed in New York City, NY.

First printing edition 2023.

Jess, Mo' Books LLC

P.O. Bx. 1808

Albrightsville, PA 18210

www.jessmobooks.com

PART: ONE

In the days when the judges ruled, there was a famine in the land. So a man from Bethlehem in Judah, together with his wife and two sons, went to live for a while in the country of Moab.

Ruth 1:1

CHAPTER
ONE

NAOMI

T he high-pitched night song of the cicadas never seemed that haunting before. Their chirping was as noticeable as one's breath, against the quiet of the after-storm. Used to the violent sounds of the inner-city Wards, most of us had never heard cicadas put on such a clatter. The sound was a deafening reminder to everyone crowded like sardines in the Superdome that the world around us continued, and we were blessed to be amongst the living. It was our lives that would never be the same.

I had lost my sense of timing...but I wasn't alone. There were thousands of people lying in the arena, all staring out of the opening in the metal roof, ripped apart by the raging winds of Hurricane Katrina. We gazed at the stars and listened for anything that sounded familiar. All afraid. All unsure. The sounds of darkness crowded us in even more, and there wasn't room left for not another thing.

It took some time, but my small family of four was finally able to move from the gathered arena area into the exhausted lobby exit. There, we bumped into a family member who was free from the chaos and bussing people to safety. He promised to return and retrieve us.

"It's just a matter of time," I continuously repeated, trying to encourage everyone. The reality was the situation looked grim. We lost everything but our lives and the clothes on our backs.

Before Katrina, the Superdome seemed like a safe place to shelter, yet it was as dangerous as any back street alley. It was a fight to survive the poor conditions, especially with my husband, Eli, in a wheelchair. He was diabetic and needed his insulin shots. The stadium lost power as soon as the storm hit, then, the backup generators quickly went down. In the ninety-degree weather, the stored rations and medications were completely wasted. The police department, FEMA, and ordinary civilians were doing their best to help. In the back of my mind, I knew for our relative, Sal, to make it back through the madness to rescue us would take a miracle. So, I did what I do best, I prayed.

CHAPTER
TWO

RAHAB

"Sal, please!" I begged, running behind my husband, attempting to keep up with his confident strides through the house. All I needed was for him to stop and listen to my reasoning. A nudge in my spirit warned me that something wasn't right. "Babe, please listen."

"Rah!" Sal finally answered, abruptly stopping, causing me to bump into him—stepping on his heels. He deeply sighed. Annoyed, he turned around and firmly held my shoulders, guiding me aside from his work path. "Listen...sweetheart. Ah understand your concern, trust me ah do—"

"If you understand—" He pinched my lips shut.

"You gon let me get a word in edgewise?" He released them, and I lowered my head, grudgingly nodding. The glooming feeling of fear was encroached upon me. A knot the size of Texas was lodged in my throat.

Although aggravated, Sal, being sensitive toward my feelings, drew me into his arms. "Now listen, ah understand ya concerns but...," he sucked his teeth and slightly shook me, "damn-it Rah dis is what ah do. I'm an officer of de law!" He pointed to the shining tin star pinned proudly on his chest. It reminded me daily that his life was constantly in danger. "Don't you understand what's happening out dere, Honey?" He started walking again, picking up an awkwardly long green duffle bag and flinging it over his shoulder.

"Of course, I do."

"Den you should know ah cain't just sit here...tiptoeing through de tulips while thousands of people are in need." Sal turned facing me, looking squarely into my wet eyes. "Dat's not even in my character...and it's not who you married either. You know me...de only thing ah cain't do is sit by and watch." He put down the awkward green bag I knew contained weaponry and pulled me close again. "Now stop all dis here. I'll be back later tonight." He kissed my forehead.

I understood what Sal was saying. My heart just didn't want to hear any of it. I pressed my face into the black aviator's jacket he wore, covered in patches from the many destinations he'd been to and started to cry.

Salmone Joshua Abrams was not only the Sheriff; he was a military man, my husband, and personal hero. I knew the notion of him staying behind during a catastrophe like Katrina to pacify me was crazy thinking.

"Come on now, Rah Sugah," he stroked my head with warm pressing hands. "Hush dis crying. Mr. Ralph is waiting out front for me."

"Sal, I'm telling you—my spirit is troubled." I wiped away the tears and gazed into his deep-set eyes. They still held a youthful spark. "You're spreading yourself thin; you've been out there once today already! You know how you always getting on me about working too hard on the farm? Well, this is the same thing. Now... I'm afraid if—" The thought of what I was saying made me shiver. I turned from him and looked out of a sizable five-pane bow window facing a meticulously groomed lawn that the storm had oversaturated. "I'm afraid if you leave, you're not coming back."

"Ma! Now dat's enough!" Our son, Boaz 'Shadow' Abrams, his father's clone, interrupted, getting up and walking over. He was lounging on the sofa watching my meltdown and standing by as usual when concerning his dad.

"No, son," Sal responded with a hand extended toward Shadow, motioning for him to stay put. "Dat's okay. Don't disrespect ya mama. She's worried is all...lak women do." He turned back to me. "Rah...if ah die taday or ta-morrah, dat's God's business, and me sitting in here or going out dere ain't gon' change dat fact." His thoughts gained traction as his attention shifted to higher things. "If death be my plight, it is what it is, and ah say thank you Lord for all you have done for me."

"You talking crazy...and that ain't even funny." I pulled from his arms, becoming angry.

"Okay, y'all both need to stop talkin' lak dis." Shadow was getting upset too, although maintaining a playful spirit like his dad. "Ma, Pa is a good man. Ain't no harm gon' come his way." He rested his hand on Sal's shoulder.

"Why, thank you, son." Sal playfully boxed Shadow's chest. They were the same height and build. "Not dat I'm expecting any trouble," he rubbed Shadow's head, rustling his curls, "but you should get dis straight. One thing ah know for certain is dat rain falls on both de just and de unjust—and dat's de God's honest truth."

"Ah know, Pa, but we ain't preaching dat sermon rite now." Sal was also the assistant pastor at his family's church, The House of Judah. He had a lot going on and was constantly pulled in every direction. "Ma would you feel better if ah went out with him...he might need some help." Shadow poked at Sal's waistline and tugged at his belt. "Dis thing growing right here...holds him back sometimes." They instantly broke out into a playful scuffle.

"That might not be such a bad idea," I added, thinking on the matter as they proceeded to wrestle with one another. *If Shadow was there, Sal would definitely be careful.* I sat at the nook facing the window that showcased acres of land carpeted in the greenest grass ever. Instantly my mind wandered back to the many family gatherings on the lawn, deeming them 'the good old days' when everyone was youthful...and living.

"Boi!" Sal yelled, confined in a headlock and drawing me back from my thoughts. "Com'on now, knucklehead! Stop!" He insisted, ending his and Shadow's fun. It only took one glance for him to acknowledge my sadness. He sighed and re-tucked his uniform shirt, returning to the business at hand. He cleared his throat.

"Son, ah need you here caring for ya mama, aint-tee, and paw-paw. I'll return once ah find Cousin Eli, his wife, and family again. He reached for his hat, sitting displaced on one of the many boxes scattered around the room. "I'll bring 'em back instead of going to Houston, okay?" Sal added, addressing Shadow but really reas-suring me while sitting the Stetson on his head in a dignified manner. He glanced my way again, worried about me too. "Why don't you, Shadow, and Tita go down to de Y on Main and help set up to shelter folks tonight. Make ya self busy. It ain't good to be sitting up in dis empty house with too many memories worrying and being sad."

My great aunt, Mary Mags, whom I fondly referred to as my grandmother, and her husband, Papa Will, had recently passed. We were sheltering from the storm in their home in Baton Rouge while helping their long-time friend and caregiver Martita, we called her Tita, to pack away the house. It was too big for her to live in alone.

"Now come on, give me some sugah 'fore ah go." Sal insisted, planting his feet, tilting his hat backward, and wrapping his arms around my waist. "Son, turn ya back, I'm fixin' to kiss ya mama up real good."

I allowed him to draw me close and I hugged him as tightly as possible. Sal had a smell that always brought me back to his arms and to the days of our youth together. We kissed, and I relaxed momentarily in the safety of his embrace. He was big and burly; you'd think no harm could come his way.

"Tante Tita!" Shadow yelled, leaving the room. "Dey in here foolin' around in ya house!"

We laughed.

"Seriously, babe, please think of us and be safe. Don't take on more than you should." I zipped up Sal's jacket and fixed the collar. It was coming down like cats and dogs out there. "I need you...and that shadow of yours," I motioned toward where our son was standing before leaving the room. "He would die without you."

Sal squeezed me tighter, bending to nuzzle and kiss my neck. "I ain't trying to leave my good thing." He moaned, patting my derriere. "Y'all go on down to the Y and keep ya self busy. And please don't let Pa overexert himself." He pecked my cheek, picked up the green bag, and turned toward the door. Mr. Ralph was patiently waiting. They had the church bus. They were shuttling people from the Superdome to the Houston Astrodome earlier. "See you later, alligator." Sal opened the door and smiled back at me before quickly leaving.

I stood in the empty room with my arms wrapped around myself, already missing his embrace. "Afterwhile, crocodile," I mouthed, not knowing how to feel.

CHAPTER
THREE

NAOMI

S eeing Sal's bright smile was better than any word I'd ever heard or spoken. I'd only met him once when Eli and I married—then, he was a young boy. Long and scrawny. His father, Pastor Josh, Eli's only uncle, married us at his church in the Bayou. Eli used to carry on about how his uncle took him hunting and fishing as a lad. His own father was MIA. The only thing he left Eli was his last name. Wiggins.

"Praise God," I shouted, noticing Sal making his way toward us through the crowd. People were pulling on him and begging for his help.

We were nearly outside of the arena, waiting amongst thousands to be bused to Houston. I didn't want to go to another stadium. However, the National Guard said that the Astrodome was fully operational and equipped for the influx of people—and Eli needed his insulin.

"Sal, we sure is glad to see you, Bubba!" Eli piped out as Sal briefly hugged his neck, then instantly joined in helping our twins, Kilion and Mahlon. We called them Junnie and Peewee. They were trying to get Eli strapped into his wheelchair and down the steps still puddled with standing water. There was no time for customary salutations.

I fought off the crowd hovering over Sal's back. His neatly pressed uniform drew everyone's attention. They wanted out, too, and I couldn't fault them. We were living in the worst conditions. The plumbing system broke down days ago, forcing people to urinate and defecate anywhere they could. Feces covered the walls. The smell was revolting. Thank goodness for the medical masks that were handed out.

"If you wanna come with us, help clear de way." Sal expressed to two big strapping young men in front of us. "We heading to Baton Rouge tho'."

"Oh, word?" they responded, then quickly yelled, "move out de way, move out de way! Police coming tru."

I fought to keep up the rear. There was nothing about me that read push over. I was a tall, big-boned woman, and the only thing stronger than my countenance was my faith. The crowd pushed, and I pushed them back harder. All I could think about was Eli's medicine and a hot shower. I wished that home was an option. We owned a compact house left behind in the Lower Ninth Ward on Delery Street. It was nothing to brag about—that area was currently underwater. We worked hard and fought so much opposition to afford the boys a decent life. A life submerged in water. I glanced at my beloved husband being wheeled through the doors of the Superdome. Even in distress, he smiled. Maybe it was his faith that kept me strong. *Poor Eli*. I pressed through.

Elimelech Wiggins was my soldier boy. We met while he was on leave in Chicago, where I was a barmaid. According to him, he saw my long legs and instantly fell in love. Eli scooped me off my

9

feet and changed my life forever. My people were originally from Florida. They migrated up north in the late '30s and ended up in Chi-town. When I met Eli, I was a Cabrini-Green project-girl, rough around the edges. He was a gentleman baptized in Southern Baptist etiquette. He brought me back to his hometown, and we raised the twins in the church the best we could under the growing criminal climate of the Lower Ninth Ward in New Orleans.

IT FELT LIKE A DREAM. The streets of downtown New Orleans looked like they teetered on the boundary of hell after Hurricane Katrina. She didn't look or feel like her old self, yet there was hardly time to take it all in. Sal was ushering us into a dingy old church bus with the words 'The House of Judah' painted in bold burgundy letters on the outside. We scarcely made the fit with the number of people he and Mr. Ralph already collected. Once again, we piled in like sardines, and Sal squeezed in amongst us. He insisted on giving Eli the front passenger seat. I guess Sal could also tell that underneath Eli's painted smile, he was in poor condition.

Eli had undergone an amputation below his knee in 2003 due to his sugar diabetes. Before that, he'd lost sight in his left eye. I feared the odds were against him, being an overweight black male in his early sixties. I didn't know what I would do without Eli. He was my rock, and I was the earth beneath him. He covered me, and I held him up.

We were setting out and on our way to a shelter in Baton Rouge when an elderly White woman appeared from nowhere and jumped in front of the bus, causing an abrupt stop. Sal, who was trying to catch his breath through an opened window from the horrendous odor that permeated the bus, yelled out to the old lady after asking if we all were okay.

"Ma'am, we ain't going to de Astrodome. We headin' to Baton Rouge!"

The older woman moved closer to the vehicle. "Please help me," she cried in a voice so faint it broke my heart. "My husband is gone, my kids are gone; I'm out here all by myself." I could hear her pleading when Sal opened the door to get out. "I don't care where I go. Please don't leave me out here."

"Sal, we don't have room!" Mr. Ralph reminded him. Not another person could fit.

Sal removed his hat and ran his hand over his head, scratching it just a little in frustration. I knew he was exhausted.

"Don't do it, ese," Mr. Ralph mumbled from the driver's seat, followed by some extra words in Spanish.

"You can have my seat, ma'am." Sal offered anyway.

"Bless your heart," the older woman answered, already climbing in despite the groaning coming from inside.

Sal shut the door and knocked on the exterior, bidding us goodbye as we drove away, leaving him in the very place none of us wanted to be. I watched from the window as he crossed the road getting involved with some other officers. There was no doubt in my mind that he wouldn't stay put as Mr. Ralph requested.

CHAPTER
FOUR

BOAZ

They say death happens in threes. All I knew at the time was that within the span of two months, I lost everyone, besides Ma, who meant anything to me. Maw-Maw Mags, Papa Will...then Pa.

Being born, bred, and buttered in the Bayou, I put on a stupid front when I should have allowed myself to cry. It was all too surreal for one person to endure. In my young mind, I said, *be strong as Pa*. So I pretended for Ma and Paw-Paw's sake. In reality, a huge chunk of myself was gone.

Ever since I can remember, I've been called Shadow. How can you be a shadow when your person is missing? My perfect image to portray. Pa and I laughed at the same jokes. Our tongues were thick with our beloved native dialect and jargon. We had the same sugary demeanor, smiling eyes, not to mention hair, hands, nose, feet, and mouth. The only thing Ma can claim is my eyes. Their blueish-gray color stands out like a sore thumb against my brown cocoa skin. They compliment Ma's golden skin tone and curly blond shrieked hair. I was my father's boy and proud of the position. I literally walked in his boots. Shadow died when Pa did, and I became known to everyone but Ma and close relatives as Boaz.

IT WAS a quarter past eight when we noticed the glaring lights from a police car parking in front of the storefront window of the YMCA's makeshift shelter. Ma had just left to take Paw-Paw home. He had been caring for the displaced all day, and his spirit languished from constant prayer. Tante Tita and I waited behind for Pa to arrive. He radioed Mr. Ralph saying he'd get a ride back with one of the officers there. Cousin Eli and his wife, who were just as stubborn and stiff-necked as Pa, refused to leave the shelter for a comfortable bed at home until Pa returned. Not even to get a shower. That wasn't the case with their sons, Junnie and Peewee. I drove them to the nearest pharmacy for Cousin Eli's medicine. After delivering it, I took them home to shower.

The twins and I were around the same age. I was nineteen at the time. They were around two or three years older and definitely from the other side of the tracks. Though scorned by the past few days' events, and perhaps humbled to silence, Peewee and Junnie quickly resurfaced from their showers, revived and wanting me to help search out the nearest weed dealer.

"Lil cuz it's needed, ya heard?" Peewee rationalized.

"Word, woadie! Ain't gon' make it without a fat blunt, forrealz," Junnie added. He was the eldest but always echoed Peewee. I felt there was something off about him.

"Sorry, guys. Ah can't help ya dere," I answered, turning up the radio in the new royal blue Dodge Ram pickup I was driving. A current news report was coming in from New Orleans. "We ain't from 'round here," I added, trying to focus on the road while attempting to listen to Mayor Nagin on the radio. I knew I wouldn't have helped the cousins even if I knew of a spot.

The twins looked disappointed. Peewee swore, slapping his knee, while Junnie expressed the same sentiment, dragging his hand down his face.

"Yeah, sorry 'bout dat, fellas. We live out on de outskirts of 'Awlins. Farmland." We were proud of that.

I had been farming since I was knee-high to a grasshopper, as Pa would say. That was the only thing he and I did differently. Pa was a lawman. I was a farmer. My folks had just purchased hundreds of acres of fertile land with a large house and storefront on site. We had outgrown our old property where Ma ran her successful homegrown organic cosmetic company. Pa was supposed to retire and join the family business. We were excited about getting ready to excavate the land when Katrina hit.

"Dang! Been two—tree days now already." Peewee continued complaining, feeling agitated about not being able to get his weed. He nervously searched the small dead town through the truck's windows as I drove down Main Street back to the Y. "Peep dis, cuz, stop o'va dere!" He pointed to a nearby liquor store.

"Word, dat's what I'm talkin' 'bout. Dat joint rite dere!" Junnie danced in the backseat, bouncing the truck.

I pulled into Clancy's Plaza, wanting to get the cousins out of my hair as quickly as possible—they reeked of trouble. The twins exited the truck, determined to get their fix, looking like 'A Scary Movie' nightmare in the quaint suburban community.

"Ahh, sugah!" Peewee paused and turned around, disappointed. "Yo, cuz...you got money?" What little they had was left behind, hidden in Cousin Eli's wheelchair. They told me that crime was rampant back at the Superdome. "We had to take turns sleeping."

I was sorry about all they'd been through, but I wasn't fixing to sponsor their habits. "Ah don't have nuttin' on me."

"Damn!" Peewee shouted with his legs and arms spread open, facing the liquor store. His posture read *Lord take me now!* He sucked his teeth. "Freak dat, dis man fitnah give me a lil' taste of sumpin!" He was wearing my clothes and Junnie was in Pa's. They looked ridiculous in the jeans pulled down under their butts. Peewee had my pants cuffed up two or three times. He was so short. "Come on, Junnie; we goin' in. Be rite back, cuz."

"Word, get us a lil' sumpin sumpin." Junnie echoed, pulling and tugging at his crotch, diddy-boppin behind his brother.

I had to laugh.

THE SHELTER WAS SO quiet you could hear a rat piss on cotton.

"It's with our deepest sympathy dat we have to announce de passing of Sheriff Salmone J. Abrams," Officer Willis said, as though practiced, handing me Pa's jacket and hat. I could hear Tante Tita standing by my side, taking short and fragile breaths. "Shadow...ya pa was a great man. He'll be missed by all," Willis continued, twisting his hands.

"No!" Tante Tita vigorously shook her head, grabbing my hand."There has to be some sort of mistake. What happened?"

"I'm not at liberty to tell all de details at dis time, ma'am...but he died in de call of duty...attempting a rescue," he explained hesitantly, as though it was being pulled out of him. Tita and I both looked at Willis wide-eyed, in a daze. Nothing registered. He exhaled and lowered his head. "Sheriff Abrams was on a roof, and...it caved." As much as Officier Willis was trying to hold his composure, his voice cracked. The officers standing on either stand of him rested their hands on his shoulders. He cleared his throat. With glassy eyes and a flared red nose he relayed, "Sheriff

Abrams died upon impact. I'm sorry, Shadow. It was just one of dem tings."

My body trembled. *Just one of them things.* My legs, as weak as a newborn colt, gave way from under me.

"Whoo!" The twins grabbed me from behind and held me up. Peewee cursed. "We got you, cuz. We got you."

I was numb. My spirit evacuated. I could physically see myself leaving the premises. The sounds of moaning were all around. *Pa was right,* I thought, wrapped in Tante Tita's embrace. *God is not a respecter of persons.* If he were, he'd known I couldn't live without mine. God had the same standards for everyone...the rain falls on both the just and the unjust. If I live to be a hundred, I'll never get over losing my dad.

CHAPTER
FIVE

NAOMI

S urvivor's guilt. I think that's what they call the inner turmoil that Eli was feeling after Cousin Sal's death. To me, it felt like we went into hiding. Eli was emotionally taxed on top of feeling weak from those days without his medication. He kept repeating, "Poor, cousin. Lord have mercy," shaking his head.

Sal's sudden death was hard for Eli to grasp. Sal had risked his life to save ours and others. And he was so young. His family was all I could think of. Shadow looked so pitiful when he left the shelter that night. We didn't even get a chance to express our regards or say goodbye. But of course, we knew that we were the last thing on his mind.

That night, we stayed at the Y surrounded by strangers spread across the floor. It didn't feel right going to the house. Eli woke up early the next morning. He rolled over and whispered in my ear, "Nay, let's go to Houston."

"Houston!" I repeated, still groggy. I hadn't slept on a mat in years. It was better than the stadium seats but I had no idea how they were going to get me off the floor. I was feeling every bit fifty-five that morning.

"Yeah, Houston," Eli repeated, shaking the boys awake. One behind him and one above his head. "Ah spoke to Mr. Ralph last night, and he said he'll be back 'round seven to pick up folks heading dere." Houston was designated a mega-center for disaster information, and Lord knows we needed a clue as to what to do to recapture our lives. We literally didn't have a pot to piss in.

Eli made up his mind. My input wasn't needed. The thought of staying in another stadium after the horror of the Superdome made me shudder to my bones. Still, Eli was being persistent.

"What about your uncle? We haven't expressed our condolences to the family yet, Eli." I asked, helping him check his blood sugar level, which was acting persistently irregular.

"Ah wanna be gon' 'fore he gets here." He sternly relayed, handing me a bin for his prick needle. "Ah can't face him. Sal should have never died." I stuck an insulin pin in Eli's stomach as he groaned silently for his cousin. Sal was ten years younger than me. I understood Eli's pain and shook off my discontent about going to the Astrodome.

"Y'all ready, boys?" I asked, attempting to get them up again. They both were up late that night on their phones, finally able to recharge them. "Let's go." I stretched both of my arms out for help off the floor. The twins grudgingly got up. "1...2...3!" I counted, rocking back and forth before they heaved. They then helped their father into his wheelchair.

. . .

PASTOR JOSH, Eli's uncle, walked in before we could get out the door. Saints never sleep.

"Where y'all going?" He looked like a lost puppy. " Ah come to take you to breakfast."

Shocked to see him, Eli stuttered, "Hey, Unk...we, we heading to Houston." He wiped his eyes, instantly moist. "You know— better opportunities set up out dere for us. Nay and ah gotta figure out what to do 'bout de house and er'rything...you know." He cleared his throat, lowering his head. I felt like we were slinking out of town with our tails in between our legs.

Pastor Josh, glassy-eyed himself, gazed over all our faces. "Wulp," he said, in a booming preacher voice, "ah can't stop you. A man's gotta do what a man's gotta do, right?" With that, he turned and held the door open for us. "Let me help you, sweet-heart." He wanted to push his nephew's wheelchair himself.

Peewee, Junnie, and I walked ahead allowing them room to speak privately. Besides, I needed a cigarette break. Badly.

It was a bright and sunny morning. It looked as though Katrina had never happened in Baton Rouge. I stood against the building and pulled out my Newports, sharing one with Junnie. Peewee didn't smoke...cigarettes, that is. He and Junnie had nasty pot habits. I smelled it in their clothes and saw it in their glazed-over eyes.

"Mawma, why we gotta go to Houston?" Peewee asked, checking out his reflection in the large storefront window of the YMCA and making any necessary adjustments. That boy knew he was sweet on himself.

"It's what ya daddy feels best for the family." I dragged on the cigarette and scratched my head. We did get cold showers that night, but there was no shampoo, and my short, thin graying hair could have used a good washing.

"Ain't nothing happening out dere for us, Maw...what we's

gon' do?" Junnie asked, picking up on his brother's anxiety. He was already rocking on his tiptoes. Junnie stayed on the balls of his feet.

"We fixin' to live," I answered, matter of factly, exhaling smoke and setting my gaze on them. No matter where we went, one thing was consistent; my faith. "As for me and my house...," I proclaimed proudly, picking up volume with each spoken word as I waited on the boys to help finish the statement. It was our thing.

"...We will serve the Lord, wherever and however." They sang, smiling, whereas they usually mocked me. The mantra took on real meaning for them in those last few days.

"That's right! We'll make it." I shifted my attention to Eli. His uncle was hunched over, hugging him. "Looks like we getting ready to go," I took my last long pull on the Newport before stamping out the butt. Mr. Ralph was there with the bus. He and Pastor Josh spoke briefly before wheeling Eli back over.

"Okay, now, y'all take care ya hear." Pastor Josh hugged me loosely around the neck...he was fragile yet strong. Though cataracts clouded his eyes, I could still see his wisdom through them. "You boys behave and make sure to help ya pa."

"Yes, sir." The twins related in unison, stepping out of the way of those boarding the bus. I hoped we wouldn't be too long. The bus crowded quickly and Eli needed a good seat.

"Nay, Unk done gave us his car," Eli blurted, sort of sniveling between words. My eyes widened, and my heart leaped.

"He what!" My face expressed my thoughts before my mouth could.

"Yoo!" The boys sang, dancing around in shock.

There was no way we were taking that poor old man's car. He was in no condition to think clearly. "Pastor Jos—"

"Ah done told you to call me Uncle," Pastor Josh insisted, giving me a sharp eye as he took my hand. His warmth sent a

20

shiver up my spine. I patted his hand and tried to put on a no-nonsense face.

"Now, Uncle, you really don't have—"

"Ah know what ah don't have to do..." he released my hand and placed his own firmly on Eli's shoulder with a knowing spirit gleaming from the corners of his smiling eyes. They twinkled like his sons. "But ah am. Y'all family and dis is my only nephew...to my onliest sister. Ah can't have y'all out here struggling to get around."

Uncle's heart was in the right place. I glanced over at the shiny gray 2000 Cadillac Seville; in immaculate condition. It was his seventieth birthday gift and definitely well kept throughout the years. A floor model couldn't have been any cleaner.

"But ya car, Uncle?"

"If y'all determined to leave, it's de least ah can do." The man had just lost his only child, and all he could do was think of us. "I'll have more cars, God willing, but ah only have one nephew," he continued, then sort of laughed. "Besides, Sal used to say ah shouldn't be driving no how." His eyes looked as if they had traveled into yesteryears with his son. "Let me pray before y'all go!" His word was final. There was no debating.

Uncle took our hands and bowed his head. He had a gentle spirit that I found comforting; we would be okay. Through his heartache and pain, his work for the kingdom never stopped.

"Father, you are lak a wing dat shelters," he said, knowing God intimately. I immediately started to tear, feeling overwhelmed by our circumstances and the presence of the Lord filling the circle between us. Even Junnie and Peewee were sniffling. We had been through so much. "Protect Eli and his family from trouble wherever dey go and keep evil far from dem no matter where dey be. There are so many things in dis world dat can bring us down..." he sighed and shook his head in sadness over his own grief. "No matter de circumstance may dey remain steadfast in You. Remove fear and bring dem peace. May de three —Father, Son, and Holy Spirit be with dem day and night. It's in our Savior's name ah pray." We all said amen, hugging Uncle as he handed the keys to Junnie, the oldest. "Y'all be safe...and when you get settled, I'll mail de title, okay?"

"Uncle, I can't tell you how thankful we are." I hugged him again, feeling awkward about the entire situation but knowing I had to speak up for Eli. He was particularly quiet. His head was held down, and he was avoiding eye contact. It's a weird thing, but he shouldered the blame for Sal's passing. In the days to follow, feelings of unworthiness and confusion settled in his spirit. We lost Eli's outgoing character to isolation.

"FORGET HOUSTON. Let's go to New York City!" Eli announced as soon as we got settled into the Caddie that smelled of a Black Ice hanging tree air freshener.

Eli needed to be far away from memories of home and family. The boys were elated. I had to be the voice of reason and convince them that we needed to go to Houston first to truly understand what we were up against regarding our livelihood. Eli was sixty-two and planning to start again in a place neither of us was familiar with. The thought frightened me. He was the head of the household, and I was accustomed to his lead. That time I felt like he was leading us out of the frying pan and into the fire.

That night we stayed in a motel instead of the Astrodome, thank goodness. One look at the crowd and Eli knew we wouldn't make it. So, we parked the car and gathered the information for those displaced by Katrina regarding our homes, insurance, victim services, and such. The Red Cross even supplied us with a contact person from New York's Disaster Response Committee to help get us settled once there. A lady named Patrice called right away and took as much information over the phone as she could. I explained Eli's condition to her and that he was a Vietnam Vet. That status usually sped up the process. She assured us that New Yorkers were doing all they could to assist New Orleans, and an apartment would soon be available.

I would miss the Ninth Ward. I'd actually been there longer than I'd lived in Chicago. It was my home. Not only was it under-water but my friends and neighbors, mostly elderly people raising their grandchildren, were scattered everywhere. Hopes of rebuilding our community were slim. A gaping emptiness was left in my heart for those left behind, but I knew we'd all make it wherever we went. As my mama used to say, "day by day and inch by inch is a cinch."

"Unbreakable" by Alicia Keys fittingly played on the radio as Junnie zoomed up the highway on a 24-hour trip snaking up the East Coast toward New York City.

CHAPTER
SIX

RUTH

"If you're so holy, Abuela, where's ya husband?" I stood above my grandmother with an erect finger angrily pushed into her face as she cowered into the sofa. This was blatant disrespect in my culture—any culture. But you don't know my grandmother. It had been sixteen years, and she still held resentment towards my mother for disgracing her with an illegitimate grandchild. And that's precisely how Abuela made me feel—illegitimate.

"You're so perfect. Where's my grandfather, huh?"

Abuela owned a small framed black and white picture of an Army man, sitting atop of her bureau chest, proudly presented on a lace doily. 'Mi bella' was signed across the handsome soldier's chest. It could have been addressed to anyone, any sweetheart from a man going off to fight for his country. To my mother and me, it was a picture belonging to a frame that perhaps Abuela picked up at some boutique along her way.

"You're a fake!" I screamed from the top of my lungs, standing in the middle of her crowded altar room filled with catholic saints, colorful glass encased candles, and the fragrant scent of tuberose.

Abuela was a Spiritualist and very strict in general. I had never seen her outside her brilliant white flowing robes. She favored Celia Cruz, but her hair was always plaited into two long silver braids, pinned up on her head like a crown, giving her round brown face dignity. Because Abuela knew plants and could communicate with spirits, everyone in the neighborhood flocked to her for advice and healing.

Mi abuela, Constanza Hermosa Maria Vega, was born in Humacao, Puerto Rico, 1935. She migrated to New York City in the 1960s with her baby girl, my mother, Abril Maria Vega. We know nothing of our family or my grandfather except for the picture of the soldier on the bureau. That's how private Abuela was. We knew everyone else's business yet nothing about hers.

There were always people in Abuela's apartment grabbing her attention from Mami. My mother used to be Abuela's doll baby—only there for appearances. She wanted her to be perfect at all times. Mami's skin was fair. Her eyes were blue. When she was younger, Abuela called her Muñequita—little doll. Mami ran from her mother's smothering into the arms of any man, plucking the strings of her heart, paying her rent and my catholic school dues.

Mami used to mask herself, posing as a White woman to pick up Caucasian suitors. My father is supposedly one of those men—at least that's what the child support checks from Greenwich, Connecticut said. I know I belong to another because my skin is as tanned as Abuela's. I am the daughter of one of the brothers that captured Mami's heart. One of the men creeping through the cursed entryway of her Bronx apartment, the pit of hell—Abuela called it. A brother from the street, too poor to pay rent but charming enough to keep Mami's bedroom door open. I watched those men when I was little, uncle this and tío that, wondering which one was my dad.

"You're a fake, Abuela—falsa! A con artist, you hear me? And the only person you love is you!" I turned with that same fury and strode out of the cramped apartment, allowing the metal door to slam shut behind me. My mother's doctors had given their final diagnoses. They said Mami only had a few months to live. Abuela was my only hope of saving her.

I marched down the narrow corridor on the third floor of Abuela's Bathgate building. The gaze of spying eyes stared out from peepholes as I took my final stance on that floor and from that building.

"What da hell are you looking at?" I yelled, shoving open the staircase door with a force I wished I could've barged Abuela's heart open with.

"Whoo!" The stranger standing on the opposite side of the door motioned with his hands out in defense. I brushed past him, giving a side-eye that burned like gasoline draws in hell. "Damn!" He uttered. "I'd hate to be on the receiving end of that storm, Beautiful." I trotted down the staircase, trembling with anger and refusing to look back.

By the time I exited the building and into the light of summer sun, the tears streaming down my face had put out any evidence of a fire...or storm. I quickly wiped my eyes and made a beeline for the bus stop, forgetting that my boyfriend was there waiting.

"Yo, hold up," William 'Buggy', sometimes, 'Liam' Felix, yelled behind me, bouncing his basketball against the pavement. Wherever Buggy went, he carried that ball. It was an extension of his arms. I guess that's why he was the number one college recruit in the city. People called him Buggy because he bugged out on the court.

"What did she say?" He didn't really have to ask. I was beet-red and walking away from the building as quickly as possible.

"Estúpida, man, I swear," I related, talking to myself. "What type of grandmother is she?"

"Yo," Buggy uttered, slowing me down by pulling on the tail of my shirt. "You gonna catch a tude or do something about it?" I stopped walking and spun around toward him, flinging my arms in the air.

"I mean, what-da-hell am I supposed to do...make her work her damn magic? She does it for everybody else," I yelled, directly to the opened third-floor window. I knew Abuela was watching. Her eyes never stopped watching. "But she can't do it for her daughter—tu hija!"

"Pay her." Buggy suggested, holding his basketball against his slender waist with a painted Cheshire cat smile on his face.

"What?" I asked, annoyed. I didn't want his help or advice; this was a family matter.

"Pay her!" he said again, and began dribbling the ball so passionately, that I could feel it's bounce against the pavement in my chest. "She only responds to money, right? Pay her." He abruptly ended the bouncing and yelled up to Abuela, "How much, old lady?"

She slammed her window with the same passion he gave his ball.

Before Buggy could finish the insult he was about to sling, I grabbed his arm. "Come on, babe," I insisted, not wanting him to take on my anger. "Forget her." I wrapped my arms around his waist, and we began walking.

Abuela hated Buggy—and not because he was a bad guy. It was because he wasn't right for me...or white for me, I should say. Buggy was Black—cocólo, prieto, she would say. It's crazy; we were both minorities of African descent. However, some of the older generations and jacked-up people on both sides, African Americans and Puerto Ricans alike, suffered from colorism. Abuela was one of them. If it ain't light, it ain't right. I think that's why I was so adamant about only dating dark-complexioned guys.

"I'm sorry about ya moms, babe." Buggy stopped walking and hugged me in the middle of the sidewalk. My mother was dying from cancer, and there was nothing I could do about it. I wanted to cry, but I was so mad the tears wouldn't come out anymore. Once Mami died, I was on my own.

"You can live with me," Buggy suggested, having a way of knowing my thoughts.

"What you talkin' 'bout, boy?" I asked, suddenly ending the hug and leading him toward the bus stop. I could see the #9 from a block away. Mami and I had been through rough times before, nothing like that, but I was used to being on my own.

Buggy and I boarded the bus, showing our Summer Youth Program counselor cards. He rested his ball between his feet and held me with one arm and the busbar with the other. I laid my forehead into Buggy's sweaty chest, which always smelled like CK One. My mind raced.

"Babe, you can stay with me upstate in da dorms," he whispered into his chest toward my head, thinking of my predicament. "You know I'm gonna have my own private suite," he bragged.

"No, Buggy. Dat ain't even gonna fly." I answered without lifting my head. "Besides, I got two more years of high school to finish, re-mem-ber?" I lifted my head and stared into his beautiful chestnut-shaped eyes. Buggy was my sweetheart. We had been friends since grade school, and that was about how long I had a crush on him. Buggy the superstar—always flossin', rockin' the latest gear, girls jockin', but my first love for real.

"Well, you can live with my moms and pops at the Brownstone." He was being relentless. I wasn't exactly your average girl either. We were a popular couple at school—the star player and head cheerleader. "After I'm gone, nobody will be at the house with them but Lo-boogie...and if she keeps getting pregnant, moms probably will need ya help." His only sister was loose in the streets. Being so close in age, Lorah and Buggy were more than siblings; they were best friends. Only he knew that she had been pregnant a few times and got rid of them.

"No, Buggy, ya moms has already done so much for me." During the school year, I washed hair at her beauty spa on the weekends when there weren't any games. "I don't wanna impose on your parents. I gotta figure this out for myself." I rested my cheek back onto his chest, staring out the window, watching as the next city block passed. That's when It dawned on me that, as much as I cared for Buggy, it seemed our romance was coming to an end. He soothed my head and planted a kiss on it before resting his chin on top.

CHAPTER
SEVEN

NAOMI

Elimelech Wiggins died on our way to New York City. By the time we reached the Jersey border, his blood sugar levels were so high that they led to diabetic ketoacidosis. Like I said before, Eli isolated himself after Cousin Sal's passing. He sat in the back of the car right next to me emitting an unpleasant fruity scent and drinking himself to death. No matter how much I pleaded, Eli wouldn't eat or take his medication. He wouldn't talk to us; he only mumbled and numbed himself with alcohol.

What should have been a twenty-four-hour trip took three days. The ride was too hard on Eli; it affected his circulation. We stopped and stayed the night in two states. He kept drinking, and he wasn't a big drinker. It was as though he wanted to die. I didn't know if it was because of Sal's death or the fear and frustration of starting over again. Looking back, I feel like he knew he was dying anyway. Whatever the reason, Eli abandoned his family.

It started with high blood sugar readings and exhaustion at the Superdome. I knew then we would end up at a hospital. The further we got up North, his symptoms progressed to vomiting and hyperventilation. Eventually, he passed out and went into a diabetic coma.

We checked Eli into a Veteran's Hospital in New Jersey and stayed nearby at an emergency VA and military housing facility. The twins never rallied together to help as much as they did in the days before and after Katrina. Something awakened in them, turning them into survivors. Before then, my boys were Frick and Frack, the moochers. They gallivanted over in the Third Ward with friends from Calliope Projects, smoking pot and doing Lord knows what else. They weren't serious about anything. Giving life a hasty lick and a promise instead of an effort to better themselves. Before the storm, Eli and I were set on putting them out of the house. We were ashamed of their behavior being a Deacon and Deaconess at Greater Zion Community Church. Then, there I was a few weeks later, at the twins' mercy. A widow. Just like Sal's wife.

After the Chaplain at the hospital prayed with the boys and me, Eli was cremated. His ashes were sent to his uncle for a proper homegoing. My heart was utterly broken, and my senses may not have been in the right place, yet my motherly instinct said, *do not go back to the murder capital.* Eli's returning to New Orleans without us was well with my soul.

"Nay, what you mean you ain't coming?" Uncle asked, his voice shaking with confusion and grief. He had not so long ago laid his son to rest. "You coloring outside of de lines, ain't you?"

"Yes, sir. I am." It was not customary; the boys and I were doing something different. "Besides, we said our goodbyes. Eli wanted to move to New York City, so the twins and I are gonna proceed." I defended our choice while charging my cell phone and smoking a cigarette, leaning against a washer at a laundromat in Southern Jersey. We were given some second-hand clothes from the Salvation Army. The boys wanted to get back on the road. Still, there was no way I was packing dirty clothes or bringing anything unclean into a new situation.

"Unk, I just can't bring my boys back to that Godforsaken place; they were getting in too much trouble. They need a fresh start." I raked my thinning hair back and closed my eyes. So, many things needed to be done, but burying my boys wasn't gonna be one of them. Peewee was too familiar with the gangstas up in the Third Ward, and Junnie followed suit. At least in a new place, knowing no one, they had a better chance. They grew up with the boys in Calliope Projects. Making new friends wasn't something Peewee fancied. And again, Junnie followed suit. It was time to lay down new roots.

"I'm sorry, Uncle..." I continued in his silence. Shadow's voice could be heard in the background playing with some kids. *At least he's laughing,* I thought, sitting down to calm my nerves. "We love and appreciate you. I just gotta think about these boys now. I gotta protect them."

"Ah understand," Uncle said, lassoing his thoughts back to the present and giving a gentle answer. "Like ah told Eli, you gotta do what you gotta do. And don't you worry, I'll be giving him a proper service." I knew he would. Eli's life insurance policy wasn't much, but the United States military put their boys away nicely.

"Thank you, Unk. Once we're settled, I'll reach out to you...I promise"

"How y'all set fuh money?" He sounded as if he wasn't solely focused on our conversation anymore. One of the kids was nearby pestering him. "Come get 'em, Shadow," he muttered with the receiver down.

"We're okay. I have a few coins squirreled away in case of emergencies." I chuckled; Uncle was such a dear man.

"You sure—don't be prideful."

"Yes, sir. Eli's disability and service check just cleared Friday."

"Okay, well, don't be shamed to reach out. Wey y'all stayin'... how much longer dey fixin' to let you stay in dat free housing?"

"We fitnah leave soon after I finish drying these clothes. Ms. Patrice, the social worker from New York, called yesterday. They found us a place."

"Well, thank God for dat good news...y'all be careful out there. Ah ain't heard too many good tings 'bout New York either."

"Yes, sir, me neither. But I got my pocket knife; I carried it this far, and I ain't scared to use it." I peeked over at my clothes. One of the dryers had stopped. "Don't forget, I'm a Cabrini-Green girl. I dare anyone to mess with me and mine." I smiled, thinking of how crazy Eli used to think I was back in the days. *You ain't no milk and cookie type woman, huh?* I laughed at the memory.

"Well, you be careful with dat too." Uncle had given up and was now entertaining the child. "I'm fixin' to go. One of my parishioners is o'va here with dey kids helping with dinner and what not."

"We will...and everything's gonna work out just as Eli hoped...what's that verse...Let us hold unswervingly to the hope we profess, for He who promised is faithful," I proclaimed, good for misquoting scripture in the wrong context but somehow always making sense of it. I may not have looked like your typical Christian mother. I smoked, drank occasionally, played cards, and gossiped on the phone (with my good friend Gladys, in particular). Still, I loved and trusted the Lord with all my heart.

"Amen!" Uncle kind of snickered. "And as long as your hope is in Him, you gon' be aw'rite!"

"Okay, Unk." I unplugged my cell from the wall, needing to get our laundry before someone touched it.

"Okay, we prayin' fuh ya."

"Yes, sir, thank you, hear. Bye, now."

The boys and I were ready. Nervous but ready. The only thing that concerned me was being lonely once they started their own lives. I didn't fancy making new friends either and still hadn't heard from any of my old ones.

Who would I play Pitty-Pat with?

CHAPTER

EIGHT

RUTH

I think I noticed him before he noticed me. He looked like the ghetto version of Usher, holding up a wall—nursing a drink that he had no interest in. He only left his spot to retrieve his flashy, simpleton-looking friend from hounding random women. I was having the same problem with my friend.

My best friend, O, short for Orpah, not Oprah, and I were at the club that night, supposedly celebrating our high school graduation. O was trying to cheer me up because my mother wasn't there to partake in the occasion.

It was 2007, and Mami had surpassed the life expectancy the doctors had given and lived to see two more years before she died. She granted me enough time to finish high school and get accepted into a college—that's a mother's love. The type of love Abuela lacked, and her magic couldn't emulate. I would miss Mami greatly. We didn't have your typical mother/daughter relationship, but she looked out for me and taught me survival. We were more like sisters because she had me so young. She never coddled me, yet I knew she loved and was proud of me.

From the moment the doctors told Mami that she had cancer, she fought like a dude in the streets. She never let me see her down; she insisted I saw her as lively. At my games, she sat off from the stands in her wheelchair and watched me cheer. She smiled and clapped when I knew she was in pain. Mami taught me banking, helped me apply for colleges, and even added me to our apartment lease. She prepared me for what we both knew was coming. All I needed was a job to pay the rent. That's what college was for—to obtain a good job. Until then, I did what I watched Mami do in the past, manipulate men for money.

"All these cute guys up in here, and you steady giving the wall play! What-da-hell, Ruth?" O complained, eying another guy. "We're supposed to be celebrating. We graduated, Bisch!" She seductively danced, groping my side, chewing gum like a cow while trying to get the guy's attention.

"Yo, move with dat!" I laughed, nudging her away. O was my alter ego. She said and did the things I thought about but would never do—not as bluntly as she did them anyway. "And how the heck am I supposed to get any play with you acting like a clown. Bozo!"

O sucked her teeth. Her latest victim was walking away. "He was cute—damn!" She laughed like, *oh well,* and sipped from my drink.

"Yoo! Get ya own!" I nudged her again. She was blocking all possibilities, especially with the cute Usher-looking fella. We had advanced to lingering peeks at each other through the crowded room.

"You just sore about Buggy." O rolled her eyes. "I don't see him up in here! I see a lot of other ballers, tho!" I sucked my teeth and made a face. She was right about Buggy; he wasn't there.

Buggy and I were still dating; I just never saw him. He texted a lot of pictures of himself...all of himself, but we could never hook up. Buggy was two years into college and just as popular and famous in Syracuse as he was in high school. Still bugging on the court, making a name for himself. The NBA was calling, but he was determined to finish his education. He was supposed to be coming home for the summer; we usually worked as counselors for the Summer Youth Program. Somehow I knew that summer would be different. I mean, various summer AAU leagues interfered with the last two. Buggy insisted that he was preparing for our future. Our future had a lot of him in it and none of me.

"Don't look now, Ruthie...but Usher Raymond is coming in at three o'clock," O warned. She pursed her lips and patted her freshly plaited braids—looking everywhere but at the guys approaching us.

"Oh, snap!" I quickly fixed myself, tugging at the white fitted dress I had on, tossed my hair, and turned just in time for a full body gaze.

"Would-cha look-a-here, Junnie," the fine caramel-colored brother with hazel eyes and hair with more waves than the ocean said, maintaining eye contact. "We got us an ice cream special." He placed himself in pleasure proximity, allowing me the chance to thoroughly check him out. "A butter pecan Rican and a chocolate deluxe."

The guy named Junnie anxiously licked his lips, rubbing his hands together. "Yum!"

I had to laugh. *They can't be serious.*

Junnie was everything I imagined from across the room. Flashy and bothersome. But the cutie spoke with a southern twang that caught me off guard. I thought he was putting on, but he was as 'bout it, 'bout it as Master P.

"Whas-up, shawty?" We stood face to face. His breath smelled of Big Red chewing gum.

O jumped in front of me. "Hey, ugly, you-cute-n-whatnot; with ya little self." She popped her gum and propped up her breasts. The fitted red mini she wore matched my white one. O and I often dressed alike. The cutie sort of snickered. He had the deepest dimples.

"Dat's nice, sweetheart...but I'm aiming at ya friend." He looked around O's shoulder and at me. "What are my chances at getting to know you?"

I rolled my neck, eyeballing him. "Slim to none." But I was intrigued.

"Whoo, you felt dat, Junnie?" He asked, shivering.

Junnie already had his arms wrapped around himself, laughing. "It's COLD up in here!"

"Freezin!" They laughed, working off of each other like a tag team duo.

I laughed again. They were comical. The cutie wasn't too cool for himself, and I liked that. "Nah, just kidding, I'm Ruth." I extended my hand over O's shoulder, throwing back my head in a spirited fashion that made my large glistening hoop earrings dance. O couldn't seem to figure out what was happening.

"Scuse me, dawlin'." The cutie motioned for O to reposition herself with his hands full of platinum and ice jewelry. Bitterly she moved, bumping into Junnie, who also was kinda hanging around waiting for his next prompting. "Ruth...you have stolen my heart, fuh sho'." The cutie smiled again, and I felt a lil something, something happening with the pace of my heartbeat.

He's Fyne!

"I'm Mahlon. Dis here is my brother, Kilion...aka Junebug. We go by Junnie and Peewee, ya heard. Representin' fuh da Crescent City." He said it as if it were to mean something to us.

Junnie giggled, getting excited and rocking on the balls of his feet. "G's for life, rowdy, tru soldiers!" He threw up street signs. "Third ward, Calliope projects. Who dat!" Junnie was about as subtle as a truck and a flop with chicks.

"I'm sorry, but did you say, Pee-wee?" O and I laughed.

"Dat's aw'rite...you can laugh—dey all do, 'til dey screaming —PEEWEE! Ya heard." He sang into his hands, then bit down on his lip, moving in closer as if he intended on showing me.

Peewee's personality took up the entire room. At the time, it was refreshing and necessary. He shined like a diamond amongst all the city brothers that night.

"So we gon' dance any n'ar time...or just keep holding up de walls?"

We danced. And by dance, I mean we really danced. Peewee wasn't like most brothers, Buggy included. They dance, grinding up on girls and bobbing their heads while we do all the work. I'm a cheerleader. I love to dance, and Peewee could really move. He left sweat equity on the dance floor that night. Like Usher, it took me a minute to get 'caught up'. The only time he left my side was to smoke his lah-lah and retrieve Junnie, who would spazz out dancing in uncontrolled uncoordinated movements.

"Stay in dat sweet spot, baebee." Peewee insisted, proceeding to show him a two-step, bringing Junnie's excitement level down. "One...two...one...two, catch dat beat, ya heard."

Peewee was a great brother. He took meticulous care of Junnie, whom I initially thought was a dipshit. After hanging around him more, I gathered there was something else wrong. But O didn't catch on. She and Junnie were like peanut butter and jelly after that night. And Peewee and I, bacon and eggs. Being with him was the first time I really enjoyed myself after Mami's passing.

We shut the club down that night, and then headed to breakfast at a 24-hour diner across the street with the munchies. I smoked so much weed I didn't know if I was coming or going. I guess that's why I felt it was okay to jump in their whip and race across the bridge back to the Bronx. I did exactly what Mami used to warn me not to do. "Don't get in a car with a stranger, and never bring a guy you just met home. They could be freakin' murderers," she used to say. But I did it, and we did it, and by the end of the date, I was screaming—PEEWEE!

CHAPTER
NINE

NAOMI

"Mawma, gimme de keys to de car?" Peewee instructed, poking his head into my room from the door. After two years of living in the city, he grew accustomed to taking the car like it was his own and brought it back, smelling like marijuana and hot butts.

"Hell no!" I yelled that morning, frustrated because the twins were going through our small stash of money like water in dixie cups—hitting the streets and eating all our food. "What you not gon' do is run ya uncle's car into the ground after he done took care of it all these years," I explained from the edge of my bed in a more rational tone—not looking up from my work. I was sorting papers, trying to get our lives in order. I could still feel Peewee's glaze, so I looked up and instantly noticed Junnie walking to the door guzzling down his fourth bottle of beer. That's when I got really irritated. It was only a little past noon.

"Junnie, if you don't put that bottle down, I'ma unscrew ya

wrist, boy!" I pushed the papers aside and got up to see what the heck was going on. Peewee quickly moved away from the door.

I stood in the doorway of my room in the small Riverdale apartment that the Disaster Relief Counsel had provided and eyed each boy from head to toe. They weren't identical but looked just alike, except one was caramel and the other chocolate. One was short and the other tall. Both were dressed to the nines that day.

"What-da-heck!" I mouthed, shocked. They were completely decked out in new fashionable attire. Nothing like the winter coats, sneakers, and clothes from Target that the Neediest Cases Fund provided.

"You lak it, Mawma?" Junnie asked, twirling around. Peewee shushed him, tapping him across the arm.

I shook my head in discontent and disgust. Peewee was up to no good. "You ain't bringing none of that up in my house! What y'all need is a job!"

Peewee was silent. I could see the frustration growing on his brow. He was wise in his own eyes, and it cost him tremendously.

"Mawma, we got jobs. We—" Peewee interrupted Junnie again. This time tapping him in the chest to shut up.

"A real job!" I reiterated. "Start living on the straight and narrow." I put my hands on my hips, getting ready to really dig in. "Instead of eating up my refrigerator and looking like a pair of hooligans!"

"Maw, not taday, ya hear." Peewee headed for the door holding up baggy jeans that slid halfway down his butt, revealing Gucci underwear.

I shook my head again. *Lord have mercy.*

"Can we please have de keys...Mawma," he continued in an annoyed tone.

"Yeah, please, Mawma," Junnie echoed, rocking on his toes. I was done.

"Hell no! Y'all outta luck today." I hoped they could see the violent rays penetrating from my eyes because I was serious. "Get out, and take the train and bus like everybody else. We live in the city now!"

When I said it, I felt it would come back to bite me in the butt. Peewee would get a car no matter what. He was not one for taking handouts or orders. I hated being stern with him. There was always an anxious feeling in the back of my mind, saying, *you shouldn't've said that. Don't say no to Peewee; he'll find another way.* And Peewee's ways were no good. He never hoped, he hustled.

Peewee and Junnie were out in those New York City streets finding trouble. They got involved in some kind of money scam. Peewee swore up and down it was a legit financing job. But I knew better. Peewee was a smart boy, too smart for his own good. His father and I called ourselves doing the right thing and got him into one of those computer programming courses at the local community college. 'Computers are the future,' they advertised. We figured that was the way to keep Peewee off the streets. He was actually good at it...maybe too good. He went to school, but nothing could keep him off the streets.

Now Junnie, that's another story. Junnie was our special boy. The doctors tried to tell Eli and me that he was on the spectrum. We rejected the report. Doctors are always trying to label our young men and boys, then doping them up with medications. I sent Junnie to regular schools with his brother. When it looked like he would sit on the sidelines of life, Peewee brought him up and out. Peewee always took extraordinary care of his twin. What he learned he taught his brother—good and bad. A double-edged sword. Before Eli and I knew it, the boys were running the streets together. Unfortunately, they were doing the same things in the city where I didn't have extra eyes and ears, letting me know what they were up to. Being clueless, I had no choice but to take their word for new employment.

"What type of financing company would employ Junnie," I questioned Peewee.

"He runs errands, Maw," he said, always having an answer and persuasive words. Nothing could explain all the shopping bags coming into the house, though. Versace this and Prada that. Jewelry, shoes, boots, sneakers, you name it, they bought it. The final straw was when Peewee parked a Benz in front of the building a few weeks later.

"It's a loaner." He explained before I could ask.

I threw up my hands. "All I can say is, your ways are always in full view of the Lord. He examines ALL your paths." Peewee gave me an *oh, Mawma* look. I waved him off because I knew he was stubborn, and his ears were too dull to hear. Peewee was up to his same old bad habits. "As a dog returns to its vomit, fools repeat their folly." Those were my final words; I went upstairs and closed my bedroom door behind me.

I STOOD naked in front of a full-length mirror, hanging from the inside of the bathroom door, staring at myself and thinking.

"Ooh, Naomi. What has come of you, chile."

I was an alright-looking sweet potato pie-colored woman in her late fifties. Overweight, but not as overweight as I had been with Eli. He loved to eat. I was learning to take it easy on the greasy. But I was lonely. Just as I had feared.

Eli was not only my husband; he was my best friend. After he unexpectedly died, I went through so many different emotions: shock, fear, and anger. Mostly I was numb. The worst feeling after losing a spouse is rolling over in bed to an empty space where they once lay. It's a fresh reminder every morning that you have to face the world alone. I had to learn how to live again, single.

Eli worked hard, up until he couldn't, but he always paid the bills. He fixed things that were broken in the house, chastised the boys, and made me feel like a woman. That day, I stood naked in front of the bathroom mirror, looking at my true self through my own eyes and not Eli's tainted view of me. He saw no wrong. He looked at me as if I were still the long-legged tenderoni he met in Chicago. The mirror told no lies. My stomach overlapped and almost covered the length of my thighs. Bat-wings waved 'hello and goodbye' whenever I lifted my arms.

"This is a sad situation." I shook my head.

Even though I complained, life in the Bronx at first wasn't that bad. I was okay, just lonely. We weren't financially strapped. Eli's small pension checks were just enough to cover the rent for our tiny apartment. Peewee tried to give me money every week, but I refused. Only the good Lord knew where it came from, and I wasn't about to take any. Instead, I perused local food pantries to make ends meet. So Peewee conned Junnie, who received monthly social security disability checks to give them to me.

"Mawma," Junnie said one day, toe-walking into the kitchen where I was preparing dinner. "Can you take my checks and buy food fuh de house?" He peeked out of the kitchen at Peewee, who was hiding in the living room, prompting him as usual. "Yeah, and, Mawma...pay some bills too...ah don't lak beans tho, don't buy beans. Okay, Maw?" He hugged my waist. "Dey give me gas." He laughed, forcing flatulence.

I didn't bat an eye. "Get from in here, boy!" I popped him with the wooden spoon in hand. He laughed again, spinning around before bouncing out of the kitchen. I went back to stirring and lapping up pot liquor. "And tell ya brother to come out from behind the sofa!"

"Okay!" Junnie laughed. "Mawma's got ya number, Peewee. Come on out,...de jig is up, woadie!"

For months, Junnie's money piled up on the edge of the dining room table until I gave in. Eventually, we opened a direct deposit account. The extra money was nice, but what's money with nothing to do?

It took me a minute, but I went out and got a job just to be around other people. I cooked and waitressed at a small soul food restaurant nearby. It was there that I met up with Ms. Patrice, the lady from Human Services, again. She came into the restaurant every Friday night for two smothered pork chop specials. Patrice was single and lived with her aging mother. We were around the same age and hit it off instantly outside of her corporate demeanor.

We first met in my apartment when the boys and I arrived in the city. Patrice welcomed us to our new home. She stayed a while as I signed off on piles of paperwork. The organization provided us with a two-bedroom apartment, a stipend check made out to a used furniture store, a Target gift card for clothes and essentials, and emergency food stamps. Patrice gave me her business card and told me to call her if I had any questions about anything. She knew we were new to the city, so she offered to take us on a tour. Patrice was a kind woman. Still, I never took her up on her offer, not until we met again at the restaurant. We became instant friends. Patrice was a welcomed friendship, but nothing like me and my BFF Gladys were.

Gladys suffered injuries after Katrina and was hospitalized. Afterward, she and her granddaughter moved to Texas with family. Weeks, maybe even a month went by before I heard from my old porch buddy. Gladys told me our homes on Delery Street in the Lower Ninth Ward, which stood side-by-side, were destroyed. The entire street, minus the cornerstone church, was gone, and so were our neighbors and friends.

"De police were finding bodies stuck on trees, hanging on fences, in rock piles. Wherever der was water, der was bodies," Gladys told me. I tried to stay away from the news. It was too much on my spirit.

After reconnecting, Gladys and I talked on the phone every day, sometimes twice. While I griped about being lonely in the Big Apple. She complained about Mr. Earl, the no-good boyfriend who treated her badly. I secretly wished he'd been found hanging on a fence.

I lit a cigarette and turned from my image in the mirror; that wasn't the Nay I knew. I stepped into a tub of hot water—slowly easing down into it while exhaling smoke. With the cigarette hanging from my lips, my head pressed against the cold tiled wall, and tears running from my eyes, I silently prayed.

Lord, please don't leave me lonely. Show me how to live again.

Two things happened the next day. Number one, after nearly two years of absence, I mustered the nerve to join the local church that Patrice attended. It took me that long to separate myself from Eli's ghost and feeling like I was betraying my old church family. Number two, Peewee and Junnie brought girlfriends home for me to meet.

CHAPTER
TEN

RUTH

"Who the hell is this?" Buggy yelled from across the street. He was parking a new 2007 Toyota Camry that he wanted to surprise me with. I was in front of my building complex pressed against Peewee, leaning on the E-Class whip he was pushing, enraptured in a goodbye kiss. Junnie and O were doing the same in the back seat.

"Who the hell is this?" Buggy repeated, getting out of the car and crossing the road. We hadn't seen each other in over a month.

"Oh, shoot!" O shouted, rapidly tapping on the window to catch our attention. "There goes Buggy!" She informed me. Junnie popped out of the car, looking gangsta and harder than I'd ever seen him look before. He was ready to defend his younger brother.

"Who dis?" Peewee asked, pushing me aside. He didn't wait for a response. He puffed himself up and grounded his feet in a solid stance in front of me, ready for an altercation. "Get in de car," he instructed from the side of his mouth as Junnie covertly handed him a piece. "We got business, Slim?" He ushered toward Buggy, making him aware that he was now strapped.

Buggy was known for bugging out, but he was not a fool; he stopped at a decent distance and looked past Peewee at me shrinking in my seat.

"Oh, I see," he directed my way, disregarding the soldier-boy lineup in front of the window. He repositioned himself to look me directly in the eyes.

"She wit a real man, bruh, ya heard," Peewee cited, egging Buggy on.

Buggy covered his mouth, nodding his head like, *okay*. "Dat's how it's going down, Ruthie? You peeling off on me because my money is soft?" He sort of stooped to the window's level with big question marks in his eyes. Ashamed, I turned my head. "Wha' di rass!" He waved his hand as if to say, *forget you*, then proceeded to blast an F-bomb before walking away. I couldn't help but be emotional. Buggy was my first love. "I'ma be makin' millions, baby—BET!" he predicted before getting in his car and speeding off.

The truth is, I was tired of playing second best to basketball. There was no doubt that Buggy would one day fulfill his goals; however, Peewee was attending to my needs in real time. Before that day, the last I had seen of Buggy was my prom night. Even then, his being there was more about making sure I didn't go with anyone else. And of course, let's not forget—his shine. After that, Buggy was a 'no-show' for everything, and he got cool with me being cool with whatever. He was out of state at a championship game during my mother's funeral. I excused him because...what else was I supposed to do? His parents and siblings stood in for him. Mr. Zee, Buggy's father, and O held my hands and passed me tissues. Buggy didn't even submit the registration forms for our

routine summer job. His tournaments were always more important. Everything took precedence over me, and I always showed
up for him.

Peewee and I had been dating for a few weeks before Buggy
even took the time to check in on me. I had stopped responding to
his texts and calls, and no doubt the word on the street was in his
ear. A few of his boys lived in my building; they turned up their
noses at Peewee and me whenever we walked in or out of the
building. Peewee could hold his own; he wasn't afraid. And I never
saw him hanging with a group of guys, either. His brother was his
backup. Although, Junnie was a whole vibe by himself.

Peewee seemed to have everything I needed, so I snubbed
Buggy and didn't turn back. I declined our usual summer gig. The
other counselors and kids were certainly going to talk and ask
questions that I didn't want to answer. As long as I collected my
so-called father's child support/bribery checks, I didn't need the
job anyway. Instead, wherever Peewee went, I followed. Why not?
Before him, I sat in the house, lonely with two Pitbulls that were
hardly worth their title. Gerbils were more intimidating than King
and Queen. They belonged to my mother, so I kept them.

Peewee wined and dined me as though I was a princess. I no
longer had to con my dates for decent meals. Peewee said, "I got
you!" All I wanted was to drink deeply of the love he said he had
for me because I didn't feel loved by anyone else...not anymore. I
followed Peewee like a deer stepping into a noose. His words were
gospel and most times outrageous.

ONE HOT SUMMER AFTERNOON, I remember waking in my bed,
panicked, after a late night of partying in Atlantic City with
Peewee and the crew. It sounded like a convention outside of my
bedroom door. There were strange voices and different ringtones

all going off at once. I quickly rolled over, but Peewee was no longer there. Nervous, I grabbed my housecoat and threw it on before quietly cracking open the door. There was a gathering of people in my living room. The apartment was full of men with foreign dialects.

I picked up the bat that Mami kept near the bed and opened the door wider, hoping that once I went off King and Queen would go off with me. No such luck. *These damn dogs.* They were snuggling up and playing nice with the invaders.

"What the heck!" I voiced as Peewee appeared from amongst the strangers, smiling. "Peewee, who-da-hell are all these people?" He had the nerve to hold up a finger, beckoning me to wait for an answer. I didn't know what was going on, yet I knew it meant trouble.

"Hello, this is a supervisor, Mr. Bankole, speaking. How might I assist you today?" I heard, tuning into one man's conversation on his phone. "Yes, yes, ma'am, I'm looking at our system right now...and I can see that you only have two more weekly install-ments to make." The brother was looking at nothing. He sat there smirking at me the entire time. "Next Friday can be your final payment!" His buttery voice rose with grand anticipation. "Yes, ma'am, I can't believe it either! Are you prepared to make a payment today?"

"Good afternoon, sleepy head," Peewee said, wrapping his arms around my waist and planting a Judas kiss on my cheek. I was in shock. All the foreign brothers ran the same line—and took information with credit and debit card numbers onto paper. They handed them to Peewee, who, before waltzing over, was on a laptop punching numbers. It was identity theft. A social engi-neering scam.

"Peewee, who are all of these men?" I asked again, less frantic but still confused.

"Relax, baebee..." He knew I loved how he said that—baebee, in his twangy accent. "Dis here is de perfect situation ah been talkin' 'bout." He removed the bat from my hand and sat it against the wall. I looked into his smiling eyes and could see the wheels of his brain spinning. Peewee was highly intelligent, yet his head was filled with useless clutter. Abuela would say, "No common sense." Always fishing for an easy fix.

"You need help paying de bills, and ah need office space." He nuzzled my neck and ran a wandering hand up my thigh. "We can help each other, bae." I wanted to say hell no as Mami would have done, but Peewee had his ways. He kissed my words away while backing me into the bedroom. "You wash my back. I wash yours." He closed the door, removed my robe, and bit down on his lip like —*it ain't nothing but a thing.* "Come here, sugah."

"I thought you said you ran a financing company?" I lightly pushed him off, turning my face from his sweet-talking kisses. I knew he was conning me. He was stealing money from people. I'd seen it done before. Peewee looked over the shoulders of unsuspecting victims as they keyed in their pin codes at ATMs. Then, Junnie, who, if he bumped against you, already owned your wallet, birth certificate, and car keys, took their debit cards. Just like that, we had extra cash!

Peewee smiled and took my hands, swinging my arms. "Ah do run a financing company...ah finance de needy...'we' da needy." He chuckled and palmed my face. "Look, baebee, all ah need is a little office space. Once we build up more revenue, I'll be out ya hair."

"I don't know, Peewee. This all sounds suspicious to me." I sat on the edge of the bed and crossed my legs and arms in the same disagreeable posture Mami would have used. I had a bad habit of submitting to wrongdoings even though I knew better. There were strong feelings of conviction, but I ignored them.

Peewee got down on a knee in front of me. "Look, we gotta

trust each other. I'm makin' big money moves. You ain't effin' with no punk. I'm out here winning!" He popped a pretend collar. "What I'm doing is for us." He dug into his pocket and pulled out a knot. "Ah can show ya better den ah can tell ya." My face lit up, and my stance softened. Peewee got up and took a seat near me on the bed, handing me the entire wad. "Why don't you call your girl O and y'all go shopping." I squealed; I had never held that amount of cash in my life. Peewee laughed, pushing my hair back so he could see my delight. "Go get ya self sumpin prudy—get ya hair and nails did too." He kissed my shoulder. "Fall through when y'all finish. I'ma take ya to meet my Mawma."

I stopped speed counting through the hundred-dollar bills to look him in his eyes. I wasn't the 'meet ya mama' type girl. I mean, my first thought when I saw all that cash was—*I'm getting a new tattoo.* I desperately wanted a barbed wire tramp stamp with the heart in the middle. Not mom material. The only moms I knew were O's and Buggy's. They were cool; then again, I knew them from when I was like ten.

"Forreal, Peewee?" I said, kinda anxious but definitely honored that he would want me to meet his family. *He must really love me.*

"Anything for you, baebee."

When your heart is in flight, it's hard to be rational. I smiled, placed the money on the bureau, and showed Peewee my appreciation just as Mami taught—say thank you to the nice man.

Sin is fun for a season. Eventually, it leads to death. Little did Peewee know, the apartment he used for business was a highway to the grave. It led down to the chambers of darkness. Nothing good was ever done there. Every scheme, every enticement, and every plot was conceived and died there. A hell pit is what Abuela called it as she watched the many men coming in and out of Mami's life through the cursed entryway.

"She-devil—diabla," Abuela used to yell toward our second-floor window in the Melrose Projects, placing candles and tuberoses against the building to ward away evil. "Come out, satan," she demanded whenever she saw me, splashing me with holy oil from the small bottles she always carried on her person. Once upon a time, when I was a little girl, she would say, "Ay, muñequita. Qué linda, niña." That was before the world took hold of my reigns. I was now like Mami to her. "Diabla!"

Then, I met Mrs. Naomi.

CHAPTER

ELEVEN

NAOMI

Every time Peewee brought that girl up in here, she looked like someone new. I swear, if I bumped into her on the streets, I would not have known who she was. That's how often she switched it up. I teased, calling her and Peewee Ken and Barbie when gossiping with Gladys on the phone.

Ruthie Mercedes Vega was one of those cute little Puerto Rican girls with the type of hair you never had to do anything with. It was long, wavy, and as black as a raven. Undoubtedly, she woke up to beautiful, tamed hair every day. Still, she played in it too much. Every time I saw her, it looked different. Sometimes curly. Sometimes straight. Sometimes twisted, other days full of braids. I was taught that if you play with your hair too much when you're older, it will run away from you.

Ruth and Peewee were both tiny cute little people sold on sin. They disappeared every Thursday night and returned most Mondays or Tuesdays loaded down with bags and looking different. Beach Ken and Barbie waltzed in the house tanned with curly hair, designer flip-flops, and a mug for Mama—Malibu. Casino Ken and Barbie arrived in furs, straight hair, shiny red bottom shoes, and a mug for Mama—Vegas. Let's see, there was Ken and Barbie on the yacht, safari, skiing, hiking, summertime, winter, and spring Ken and Barbie. You name it, they did it, and I got the mug to prove it. Poor old Mama was supposed to believe Peewee worked a simple 'financing job' traveling the world with hoodrat Barbie.

My Junnie was too nervous about flying. He laid around miserable while Peewee was away. He did, however, tiptoe out of the house every now and then to bounce around on Miss O. She was a loud, nasty-mouthed, uncouth lil girl—with the prettiest face. You couldn't see it past that mouth of hers. 'Mouth-all-mighty,' that's what I called her. You couldn't say anything without O putting her two cents in it. She made me second guess my cussin' that's for sure. She led Junnie around by his nose so much that it got to the point that I didn't realize I had twins anymore. It was Junnie and O and Peewee and Ruth.

"Mawma, I'd lak you to meet my girl."

Peewee hadn't brought a girl home since high school. I sat in the kitchen on the phone, shocked with my mouth open.

"Hey, Gladys, I'm a call you back. Let me go see what Frick and Frack brought up in here," I whispered hurriedly. "Okay, girl, bye."

"Mawma! Dis here my lady, too! Her name is O!" Junnie added, grabbing the girl tautly around the shoulders. She nudged him away just as aggressively.

"Boy!" she yelled, pulling her braids around the other way. Junnie had snatched them up in his embrace. "You play too much!" She rolled her eyes then introduced herself. "Hey, Nay. I'm Orpah Alizé Collins."

Did she just call me Nay? My eyes widened. *She better put a handle on that name.* I gave a look of disapproval that didn't phase her. She tapped her scalp and walked toward me with an outstretched hand. We briefly shook hands before Miss O wandered off exploring.

"Ooh! This is niice!" She complimented our small and neatly decorated apartment. "How much is ya rent? I gotta tell my muh'va about this. There's too many crackheads where we live." She proceeded to whip out her cell and dialed a number. "Junnie, baby, where's ya room? Hey, Mommy...guess what?"

I later found out that Miss O and her family moved around a lot—her mother used to be one of those crackheads.

"Close ya mouth, Mawma." Peewee laughed, "Dat's, O—she good people. She speaks her mind...lak you!"

I made a whistling sound. "Well, shoot, if I'm like that, I need to calm down. She plain old—"

"Ahh, Mawma, dis here Ruth."

"Hi, Miz'Wiggins." The chile smiled, extending her hand. I shook it, glancing over her outfit and skinning up my face. She and the fake Oprah looked like who-done-it and why in matching poom-poom shorts as fitting as skin.

"Y'all staying for supper," I asked, turning back to the safety of my kitchen. I had nothing nice to say.

AFTER THAT, Ruth and O showed up with the boys every time they came home. Like the boys, they didn't stay long. I cooked, and they ate. They had good appetites. That was something I appreciated. I enjoyed feeding and watching people eat. It was my love language. Getting a kind word from me was like pulling teeth, but

I'd bake you a slamming red velvet cake or apple pie in a minute. It wasn't that I was mean. I swear I was a God-fearing Christian. I wasn't created to be understood, just loved.

When Ruth and O came into my life, I had already been through a few rough years, and even though Peewee and Junnie were pains in the butt, they were all I had left. I felt the Lord was taking everything I loved away. He gave to take away. I read the Word. I prayed and went to church. *Why are You punishing me,* I often wondered. Ruth and Orpah, with their faces full of the devil's paint, were luring my boys away, and I couldn't help but wear my anger.

It's odd, but somewhere below the surface of my discontent, I knew differently. Somewhere under misery, something else was taking place. Even though I didn't show it, I knew those girls and I were kindred spirits. Somehow, we needed each other. Ruth more than O. The more I tried to hate them, the Lord drew me nigh.

That Miss O was a pain for sure, but she had a huge helping spirit. She bombarded my house with her bigger-than-life presence and helped me to apply for things I needed but was too ashamed to tell Patrice I didn't have—like food sometimes. I absolutely refused to take anything from Peewee. After a few well-appreciated assisted living years in New York, everything increased. Our rent went way up, and we had to pay for our own utilities. I guess the city felt we weren't as needy anymore. But Miss O knew the system.

"Being given food stamps and applying for food stamps are two different things," I told her.

"Why," Miss O asked. "Didn't you say your husband fought for this country? Why the hell can't you get food stamps and not worry about ya effin' lights being turned off!"

"What'd you say?" I regularly asked, trying to get Miss Thang to clean up her act.

"Ion know?" She'd lie, looking innocent, batting her eyes.

"Lil girl, you need to set a guard over that mouth of yours and keep watch over the door of ya lips." *Mannish, smart-mouth kid.* Yet she was wonderful. Miss O went head to head with the insurance company that was dragging their feet on giving me the claim money from our house in the Lower Ninth Ward.

Then, there was Ruth. She was a tough cookie to crumble. She reminded me a lot of myself from back in the day, a pretty girl trying to get over on her looks.

"Charm is deceptive, and beauty is fleeting." I reminded her every time she left my house with that cute little pierced nose of hers stuck up in the air. She hated me saying that. She hated hearing anything that resembled the truth. Maybe she feared her own possibilities, I don't know. Yet I couldn't help but try to help her. There was something about Ruth's eyes; they were wide and endless as doves. I knew there was more to thug life Barbie than she was putting on—her and her sidekick—the ghetto Oprah. I was rough on them in the beginning, but I liked them well enough...in my own way.

"Don't y'all have a home somewhere?" I always said when it was time to leave. There was gonna be no shacking-up in my house.

"Mawma, can dey stay? It's cold outside, and it's late." Peewee had the nerve to ask. He and Ms. Ruth were curled up so tight on my sofa watching movies they looked like one person.

"It's 'bout ta snow out der, Mawma. Weatherman said so. Winter storm," Junnie added, with his head on Miss O's lap. She was playing in his ears and face, popping bumps and whatnot. I turned on the living room lights.

"Time to go!" I stood my ground with my hands on my hips. "Ain't gon' be none of this in my house. You don't have to go home, but ya surely gotta get up outta here." I poorly mimicked

Martin. Miss O had me watching those silly reruns. She laughed.

"Okay, okay, Miz'Nay, we going. I got something to do in the morning anyway. Get up, babe." She nudged Junnie, but he didn't move. He could be defiant like that at times. "MOVE, YA ROCK!" She yelled, whacking him across the head and standing before he could. I cringed, but I couldn't have those young folks running my house and trying to take over.

Eli had set standards for the boys, and every day that he was gone, they got worse. And I felt myself slipping back into my old Cabrini-Green habits where anything goes. I couldn't wait for the kids to leave so I could close myself up in the room with a bag of chips, late-night TV, and peach brandy—if it was handy, or beer if it was near. Don't judge me. I was going through something.

I threw the girls sweaters to put on under their thin fancy designer coats. "Y'all be safe!" I pushed and held the front door open. It was cold out there. Even from the sixth floor, I could feel the hawk swooping around my ankles. I clenched my housecoat under my chin and crossed my legs. "Wear ya seatbelts." Peewee rolled his eyes. "Pick up ya pants, son, before you trip in the snow." If looks could kill. I didn't care, though. *Ain't causing me a lick of sleep.* "Love you too, son."

"Love you, Mawma."

That Peewee, he was only getting worse. That's what happens when you let sin sit comfortably in your life for too long. He rose early every morning to run after money, drinks, and weed and stayed up late every night until he was inflamed with it all. Ruth, she hung in there, but it seemed Ken and Barbie weren't going to make it.

CHAPTER
TWELVE

RUTH

I was sick of her curt remarks and exasperating looks. Unable to refrain my tongue, I returned her attitude unabashedly.

"I got ya Barbie doll!"

Mrs. Naomi made me feel stupid and lazy. She hated me.

"No, she doesn't, Bae," Peewee insisted. "She feeds you don't she...and what's dat in ya hand?"

"Her big-azz sweater," I answered, sucking my teeth and rolling my eyes. I had two of them at home that I hadn't returned.

Peewee sort of chuckled. "Don't be talking 'bout my mama's sweaters!" He placed his arm around my shoulder, drawing me in, as we walked out of the building, carefully through the snow, and into his heated car. "Trust me, she laks you. She ain't want you catching cold."

"Whatever." I laughed, "if this is her way of liking me, who needs enemies."

Peewee was right, though. Mrs. Naomi had a strange way of

showing affection. Instead, she carried misery on the arches of her sloped shoulders, yet she was oiled with a sensitive spirit—though I rarely caught a glimpse. What I got was a saggy armed Baptist woman who could put the fear of the Lord in you on the drop of a dime because she obtained the fear of the Lord herself. Her famous line was, "you ain't bringing none of that up in my house," and she meant it.

Mrs. Naomi had an endless encyclopedia of quotes. She was always slinging biblical life hacks meant to instantly correct any misbehavior—mostly mine and Peewee's. She mumbled her clichés as she stood over a pot at the stove in her well-stocked kitchen, gossiping on the phone and lapping at soup or something.

"A lady never rests her elbows on the table..." she happened to mention, peeping out at us, "...and she always crosses her legs at the ankles." She was irritatingly perfect. I ignored her and annoyed her. "If you wallow with dogs, you get up with fleas."

"So, I'm a dog now?" I pushed away from the dinner table and stood ready to pop off. Peewee grabbed my arm.

"Bae, dat ain't you," he excused her yet again because she was talking on the phone; still, I felt her direction. "Just ignore all dat. Da, da, da—dat's all it is." He mimicked chit-chatter with his hand, and I plopped down in my seat, angrily pushing my plate away. Mrs. Naomi could cook. Her food was always num-num. However, the price wasn't worth the aggravation. I only ate there because of Peewee.

"All I know is," she spoke to no one in particular, hanging up the phone and strutting into the dining area with a pompous gait, carrying an overstuffed plate to the table. "Sin will take you farther than you wanna go, keep you longer than you wanna stay, and cost you more than you wanna pay." She placed the plate down at her seat. "If you live long enough, your day will come...and that's a fact, jack." She gave Peewee a mother's look.

Peewee shook his head and sucked his teeth, giving her a side-eye. "Man...really, Maw?" He pushed his plate away, too. "Why are you always making erroneous and frivolous assumptions 'bout me and mine?" Mrs. Naomi slammed down the hot sauce and settled her fist on her hips.

"Don't be coming up in here picking dem big words up out ya-azz, boy." She knew Peewee's hand and called his bluff. But Peewee wasn't all that bad. Yeah, he did run scams. What Mrs. Naomi didn't know was that we were working on funding legit businesses too. Peewee was taking his sweet time—still he understood that his time was running out on getting over. He wanted better for himself. We were making plans to get married and start a family.

"Peewee, there are six things the Lord hates—seven that are detestable to Him." Mrs. Naomi took her seat at the head of the table and intertwined her thick fingers placed across her bosom.

Peewee got up, slapping his hands against his head and spinning in frustration. "MAWMA, I KNOW!" No doubt Mrs. Naomi beat it into his head.

"Haughty eyes...," she continued, unbothered by his display.

"Here we go." Peewee pulled out his seat and sat facing her, readying for the challenge.

"A lying tongue. Hands that shed innocent blood." She rocked her head and pointed a blaming finger. "A heart that devises wicked schemes." Peewee clenched the bridge of his nose and closed his eyes. Mrs. Naomi was hitting a raw nerve. "Feet that are quick to rush into evil. A false witness who pours out lies—"

Peewee leaned in and rested his hands on either side of his mother's shoulders, looking her directly in the eyes, and said along with her, "...and a person who stirs up conflict in the community." Mrs. Naomi sort of smirked, her years of brain-washing were heard.

I hated the quotes and her holier-than-thou attitude; still, even I felt that one. She was right about my boo. I loved Peewee like nobody's business, but he was definitely on the wrong path. I followed him all those years because he gave me what no one else had ever given me before—all his attention and money.

"As for me and my house…," Mrs. Naomi sang with elevated tension, "we will serve the Lord, whenever and however," she insisted, using a gentler tone.

"I'm trying, Mawma…if ah could just open dis club, I'll stop all dis foolishness."

Peewee had dreams of opening his own establishment. During our travels, we frequented different nightclubs. Peewee was confident that what New York City needed was a New Orleans-influenced spot, featuring his beloved bounce music. Crescent City is what he wanted it called.

It had been ten years since Katrina, and there were plenty of misplaced New Orleanians in the city. A club like Crescent City, hosting weekly parties, would help them feel more at home. Mrs. Naomi had finally received her property compensation, and even though it wasn't as much as they'd all hoped, it had been working Peewee's nerves to get his hands on some of it. The insurance company pegged the payout down to home value rather than the cost to rebuild. It left many homeowners short of the money needed for new residences. Mrs. Naomi had big plans to rebuild her home in New Orleans, right next to the home of the woman she spoke with on the phone daily. There was no chance of Peewee getting that money.

. . .

YEARS PASSED, and I still could do nothing right. Peewee was no better. I may have understood or even respected if Mrs. Naomi had said, "y'all on the wrong path, let's sit down and talk," but all she did was preach to us while babying Junnie. And mind you, Junnie followed right behind his brother. His hands were just as dirty. Just because he was mildly atypical, Mrs. Naomi deemed that he needed her. His mind at times was as a child's, very impressionable. But I bet she never gathered that another woman would take her place. O did.

O could handle Mrs. Naomi. To O and Junnie, their ignorance was bliss. Mrs. Naomi tried her best to mess with them, and they left her astonished with their blasé attitudes. Then, O got pregnant.

CHAPTER
THIRTEEN

NAOMI

When I looked up ten years had passed since Katrina, and Junnie was about to be a father. He was a baby himself. If I were an atomic bomb, I would have blown half of New York City away. I was that mad.

How in the world did this happen?

"I'm pregnant, Miz'Nay," O announced, just like that. "And when Junnie and I...and Ruth and Peewee get married...," she spoke in a slow, monotone manner making sure that I understood each word. I was sixty-five years old. Those kids treated me as though I was ninety-one and simple-minded. Miss O was the ringleader. "We all feel it best that we move in with you to save money." I knew they sent O to talk to me because I was hot-tempered. Her brazen nonchalant approach always caught me off guard. That chile's mouth was as deep as a pit. I got lost in her words. To make it worse, she was now pregnant with me and Eli's blood. *What could I do?*

Miss O went down the line as to why their moving in made sense. I had stopped working at the restaurant. All that standing was brutal on my old knees and back, so I was collecting Eli's social security. O helped me with that too. Peewee and Junnie had ended their 'financing business'—or got in trouble, I don't know, but the trips around the world suddenly stopped. I was glad to see the boys had come to their senses—then again, if it ain't one thing, it's another. They were eager to move the girls into our small apartment and I felt like I was being pushed out of the way.

Peewee and Ruth practically lived together already. Ruth aged out of child support once she finally finished college. For a while there, she was becoming a professional student. However, she did obtain quite a few degrees. When Peewee ended his hustle, I guess there was no more income for either of them. They, along with the dogs—Queen and King, were homeless. Still, there was no way I was living with two pitbulls. I didn't care how sweet they all said they were.

"I put in for a three-bedroom apartment with housing for you a while ago. It should come through soon...hopefully." Miss O continued. I stared at her with wide eyes and an open mouth.

The audacity!

She proceeded in a point-blank manner, no matter what disapproving grunt or gesture I made. "We need room for the baby and dogs, Miz'Nay! Junnie and I could move in with my moms, but it's already overcrowded over there." She leaned in like we were chopping it up. "You know my brother, Sisco...he and his girl just had their third baby...so that's out. But let me tell you, once Peewee and Junnie's new business kicks off," she reached out and lightly pushed my shoulder, "chile, we'll be able to take care of everything...now that's a win-win!" She ended rather perky-like, grasping her hands into a clap. "You using that rosemary on ya edges like I told you, aren't you?" She slid that in, sort of whispering but not. "Dey growing." She winked.

I tugged my headscarf down and cleared my throat. "Are you done, Miss Thang?" O crossed her ankles and laid back into the comfort of my sofa, rubbing her flat stomach and making a winded sound—reminding me of her condition. "First off!" I whipped out a cigarette because I needed one.

"Oh hellz no, Miz'Nay!" She clasped my hand. "You know you can't smoke around me—I'm pregnant." If my eyes could have launched missiles, she would have disintegrated.

"Listen, here! Ain't gon' be none of this up in my house!" I rolled my neck, getting up. Junnie, Peewee, and Ruth were huddled in a corner out of harm's way. Miss O didn't flinch.

"Now, now, Miz'Nay...watch your blood pressure." I fixed my hands to wring her neck.

"Mawma!" Peewee yelled, coming out of hiding. "Look, ah know dat was a lot to take in...but honest we trying to do da right thang."

"Peewee, how the heck you let Junnie get this one pregnant." I was so mad my voice cracked.

"Ah loves O...she my Queen," Junnie interjected, pouncing from the corner on his toes. "We fixin' to get married." Peewee rested his hand on his brother's shoulder to stop him from talking. He knew a soothing tongue was needed.

"Oh, Lord." I had to sit down; I was seeing double.

"Listen, how 'bout we go to Easter service with you tomorrow...den afterward we can talk things o'va dinner. My treat."

Lord, this is really happening.

Peewee and Junnie hadn't been to church since Eli passed. He used to make them go every Sunday, or else they weren't allowed back in the house. "A family that prays together stays together," he always said.

Maybe that's what's missing. I had fallen into the trap of bitterness, feeling sorry for myself, and lost sight of the boys and my faith. Of course there was my overindulgence in my guilty pleasure of nightcaps, which had turned into wine o'clock any time of the day. My mother used to tell my father, "Wine is a mocker and beer a brawler. Whoever is led astray by them is not wise."

And you call yourself a Christian? I felt ashamed of myself. I looked around at the kids' faces; each was clinched in distress. My answer seemed to determine their future. *Maybe Peewee is trying to get his life together? I guess we all messed up.*

THE BOYS WERE serious about starting a business and getting married. Well, at least Peewee was. And he knew precisely how to soften me up toward his plans. Seafood. After Easter service, we waited an hour on City Island to be seated at Sammy's Fish Box for my favorite. King crab legs.

"Mawma, if ah can't get dat money from you...well den, we can't support our families...and ain't no way I'm 'bout to let dat happen. Ah loves Ruth, we want babies." Peewee was like his dad in that way, a one-woman man. I never had to worry about Eli stepping out on me. He fell hard, and so did Peewee. "If I can't get the money from you," Peewee continued, leaning back in his seat. He had hardly touched his plate. "I'ma have to go into business with Skee Ball 'em."

I stopped eating, dredging my lump crab meat through garlic butter. Instantly, my face collapsed into a scowl of disappointment and worry. Skee Ball was from Calliope Projects. He was the heartless thug that Peewee grew up with. Gladys had warned me that he was out of jail. Trusting Skee was like leaning on a spider's web. "He's talkin' 'bout coming to New York for a fresh start...you know we homies."

"Tru soldiers! Brothers stuntin' fo' life!" Junnie tuned in with garlic butter juices running down his chin. He and Peewee pounded fists across the table.

O sighed. "Come here, baby," she wiped Junnie's mouth with her greasy napkin and sucked at her claw-like fingernails.

"Peewee, now I don't wanna hear none of that foolishness." I had lost my appetite and yanked off my plastic bib. "Skee is bad news. I don't want you and Junnie hanging 'round him. Bad company corrupts even the best of character."

"Well, Mawma, won't you and daddy de ones who taught us de importance of staying de course...never quitting on our dreams." He threw me a condescending look. "You said, once a task has just begun, never leave it 'til it's done..." I lowered and shook my head. Don't you hate when your own words come back on you? "Be de labor great or small," Peewee continued, nailing in his point, "do it well or not at all...well ah have a great opportunity to turn my life around and support my wife-to-be and get up out ya house. Ah need for dis to happen FOR US." He sat up and put his arm around Ruth's waist as she continued working on sucking the meat from her crab legs.

Without looking up, she grumbled, "Mmhm." I knew this idea was all Peewee. Ruth looked like she was fed up.

"Ruthie got her degree in business management—I'm telling you, Mawma, we gotta fair chance." He waited patiently for Ruth to remove a firm cluster of meat from its casing and then stole the first bite. She gave him an evil eye and nudged him off. Peewee devilishly laughed, sitting up and bringing his plate back. "We've been savin-n-everything, Maw. I'm telling you, we serious. All we need is your portion to make it all work."

"Peewee...son. I admonish you. I beseech thee or whatever

else King James version word I can use to impress upon you." I reached across the table and laid my hands down, palms up. "I beg of you...do not get into business with Skee Ball 'em...I'll give you what you want." The dark cloud encompassing the table relinquished. I knew how demanding and unpleasant Peewee could be when he couldn't get his way. I could only imagine the tightrope walk he was putting them all through. Especially Ruth. He stretched his hands across the table to meet mine, smiling. "Just know it's all we have, son." I reminded him, squeezing his hands and releasing my dream of returning home to Delery Street to rebuild. "Do not run this family into the ground."

"Mawma, I'll die fur ah do dat."

CHAPTER
FOURTEEN

RUTH

Mami used to have a friend named Ms. Louis. When she was sick, Ms. Louis was the one who took her to her doctor's appointments and helped to manage her medication. Their friendship wasn't like me and O's, or Mrs. Naomi and her phone friend for that matter. They didn't have to speak every day. Before Mami got sick, they spoke once every other month or a few times a year. But whenever they hooked up, it was like magic. They took off where they left off, laughing and remembering good times. They were always there for each other.

Ms. Louis was very religious, not like Abuela. She didn't claim healing powers, nor did she claim wisdom in her words like Mrs. Naomi. Ms. Louis was a quiet spirit. All she had was a Bible and her prayers. With that, she managed to tame the wild beast that my mother was. She led Mami into peace before her passing. Mami no longer worried about dying or where she was going, as I did for her. She knew we would meet again.

"Get right with God, Mamita," she often said, not explaining but making it seem expedient that I did.

It's funny; my mother and I were never that close. She wasn't a coddler. Like Mrs. Naomi, she handed out 'I love yous' sparingly. It was a given. I knew she loved me. In the finality of her life, everything she did and said became significant to me. I cherished her words because they floated away. I noticed things that before didn't matter. We laughed alike. We both had cowlicks and baby feet. Mami was frisky—many would say whorish. No, she was resilient and wise. Her ability to grasp life and suck out its joy deemed her reckless. I'll admit, there were many times when I would've preferred a mother over the overaged sister she pretended to be. There was no off button. I guess I envied the peace Ms. Louis impacted upon her. At the time, my life was spiraling along with Mami's, and I wanted that sense of eternal security. Yet, I shunned Ms. Louis when she came around after Mami's death—trying to check in and witness to me. By then, I had fallen into my own misery. I didn't want anyone but O around. That's why meeting Peewee was a ray of light. He wooed me from the jaws of distress.

Peewee and I weren't perfect people. Our relationship was perfect for us. We both had empty spaces that needed filling and were both people who loved the idea of being in love. Although flawed, I was Peewee's Queen, and he was definitely a one-queen man. It was his own low self-esteem that kept him questioning my loyalty. Peewee accused me of cheating so many times that he made me believe I was. I couldn't help that men found me attractive. In the words of Mrs. Naomi, I'm stacked like a brick house. That I owe to Abuela's genes and Mami's secret recipe. I used to be skinny growing up. Every day when I came home from school, Mami had a glass of ponche de malta with a straw waiting on the counter for me.

"No daughter-of-mine will be walking around looking like ah Olive Oyl."

Mami's high protein drink helped me to gain weight, and those men—all they saw was a big butt and a smile. Peewee loved me. However, he was no longer the man I fell in love with.

It wouldn't be a lie to say that Peewee was a bit of a narcissist and suffered from a Napoleon complex. He felt taller standing on his wallet. Everywhere we went, he flashed money, looks, and things. When other men looked at me, instead of taking it as a compliment as Buggy did, he confronted them with violent outbursts and veiled threats. After a while, it became my fault. I was flirting. Peewee was volatile. He allowed his emotions to change his character and became the stuffed shirt that loomed around, controlling my life. I'm a Latina from the Bronx through and through. I was born with my heart on my sleeve, but I also have a fire in my soul. The older I got, the less I tolerated Peewee's manipulation.

"Yo, Ion like dat!" I yelled whenever he attempted to belittle me out of my self-confidence by accusing me of everything under the sun. The professors at school wanted me. I was too flirty with the Arab at the corner store. My chatty Uber driver had peeping eyes.

"Well, if you didn't wear dem damn booty-cutters, we wouldn't have dis here problem—now would we? Who you tryin' to impress, and why it ain't me?"

"Peewee, you know you my everything. All I do is for you." That's how it started. Before I knew it, he had me dressing in loose clothes and wearing less make-up. Mrs. Naomi knew her son well, and even though we were at odds more times than not, she stuck up for me.

"Bologna!" She would say. "Boy, you oughta-be-shamed!" She interrupted, coming out of her room with an empty container of

Häagen-Dazs Vanilla Swiss Almond ice cream in hand. "Peewee, you one conceited and black-hearted chile. You the one who wanted a worldly type woman—that's what you got!" She stood in between Peewee and me. I was nearly in tears. "Lil Miss Thang has been with you all these years. Why are you insisting on ruining it now? It ain't her, son. It's you! Why aren't you enough for yourself? You know what they say, an ego ain't nothing but over-dressed insecurities."

In private, Mrs. Naomi argued with me and O over less being more. "There are a million women out there with big butts." She hated our attire yet always had our backs when the guys came down on us. "What's wrong with you hot-tailed girls nowadays is you too quick to show a man what he can get...but you don't wanna make 'em imagine what he can have." Ms. Nay swore she knew from experience. "If it ain't 'you' they want from the get-go...trust me, honey, they ain't worth having."

I didn't know if she was right or wrong; I was taught differently. All the women I knew obtained their love interests with their assets. There was one thing I did know, I was tired of feeling wrong for living comfortably in my skin.

Mrs. Naomi wasn't all that bad, not as before. We could actually sit in a room and have a decent conversation. Food was our love language. When I helped her cook, we were buddies. And if she fed me, I dropped all of Peewee's dirt. Skee Ball wasn't 'thinking' of coming to New York City. He was already there, and I hated him.

I wasn't used to Peewee hanging around other men. Junnie was his only comrade. With Skee, Peewee wasn't as dominant. He wasn't the alpha male anymore. And the way that Skee looked at me! If a look was a broken condom, I would've been pregnant by him. His gaze was nas-tee. It made me feel dirty, and Peewee said absolutely nothing. I was supposed to be involved in the development of Crescent City. Yet, with Skee Ball there, Peewee preferred I stayed away. Skee wanted a private gambling room, strippers, and a hookah bar. His vision ran a tab on our dream. That's where Mrs. Naomi's money came in; Peewee had to oblige Skee's plans. He was the big promoter. His name carried weight. We found ourselves in the hole with Skee around.

Then, there was that Easter church service that changed our circumstances and my life in general.

"THE FIRST PLACE we lose the battle is in our minds." That's how the pastor started his sermon.

That statement hit like a brick wall. I had swum around for years in a sea of meaninglessness, searching for myself and yearning for vague hope. I felt like I was running in the dark. Unsure of the space I occupied in this world. It started way before Mami became ill—maybe even as a little girl looking for a father. It all lingered over into my relationship with Peewee. We were always running, traveling here and there, and doing this and that. After a while, I didn't know what we were doing or why. Vacations are supposed to be relaxing—defusing, fun. We vacationed for show, opportunity—the Vine. Another reason to floss. It took me a minute to realize that it was almost like crackhead behavior. Peewee and I were obviously attempting to fill a spiritual void with external things. *How could that be*? I barely wanted to know myself.

"Such are the paths of all who go after ill-gotten gain...it takes away the life of those who get it." The preacher continued. "How long will you love your simple ways? How long will mockers delight in mockery, and fools hate knowledge? Repent at my rebuke!" He shouted, startling me. "Whenever you feel a lack in your spirit...it's because you're not connecting with God...it's not the need to acquire more things." It was as though he was speaking specifically to Peewee and me.

Indeed, Mrs. Naomi had preached something similar; that day, it hit differently. We had heard with new ears. At least I did. I was growing tired of STUFF; I wanted roots...family. I was twenty-six years old and had been with Peewee for eight. The light in my head was turned on—and it wasn't the artificial lighting of flashy city living either. It was the illumination of a dark place within— the part of me that wanted to check out when Mami died. I sat quietly in the church with my mind as still as a pool of water, rippled only by the touch of the Holy Spirit.

"Baebee, you okay?" Peewee asked, trying to console me. The ripples had turned to waves of uncontrolled weeping. "You wanna go, babe?"

"Shhh!" Mrs. Naomi insisted with a knowingness in her eye. "God is moving. Leave her be."

Peewee gave me a fleeting glance before clasping his hands over his mouth in concern and disbelief.

I was too young to understand then; today, I fully know. The Holy Spirit moved me to a place of understanding, worship, and praise. My soul was touched, and my tears expressed what my mouth had not yet learned to do—thank Him!

"One day, we'll all be heading to that great place in the sky— where it's always howdy-howdy and never goodbye." The pastor concluded. "Will I meet you there?"

That's what Mami wanted me to get.

FIFTEEN

RUTH

I will never forget March 27, 2016. It was the beginning of an end for me. The day I decided, despite everything, to change my life and shift gears. Peewee, Junnie, and I started attending church regularly with Mrs. Naomi, and she was more than delighted. Even O went from time to time and enjoyed herself. She dressed nicely with big church hats flopped over her head, flaunting her baby bump. Peewee and I really leaned into the word. He said the services were reminiscent of his childhood church. It reminded him of his father and upbringing. We took bible study classes and, along with Junnie, were baptized. O turned up her nose.

"Oh hellz no, I'll pass! Everybody been up in there. I can't risk an infection." She promised to revisit the idea after the baby was born.

A few weeks later, Peewee and I said 'I do' in front of a Justice of the Peace. Junnie and O stood as our witnesses, and we stood as theirs. The men wore black tuxedos, burgundy silk vests, and bow ties to match our bouquets. O and I found cute cream-colored dresses—one in a mermaid cut, the other a triumph but both strapless. Mrs. Naomi was there. She cried the entire time. I couldn't figure out if she was happy or sad because she smiled through her tears. I invited Abuela, trying to make amends. She was a no-show, and I couldn't say I blamed her after our last altercation. She talked about Peewee like he was dirt.

"The other one," she said, "the cucaracha. He was better than this charlatán." Needless to say, despite my newly found faith, I tore her a new one.

Peewee and I were trying. We had more arguments than I care to admit, but we were trying to turn over new leaves. Peewee wanted to be more than a hustler. He deemed himself a business-man. We both did. We had ideas for the club that hadn't been explored. I felt the addition of a New Orleans fast food menu would bring in more revenue, and we could rent out the space for private events. A theme drink, one exclusive to the venue, like the Hurricane to New Orleans, would've been brilliant. Peewee and I explored clubs around the world. If we learned anything, we learned that 'atmosphere' is magic. An internet-worthy experi-ence. We needed a solid social media presence. Pics upon pics and more pics. More than anything, we needed to get rid of Skee Ball.

Soon after our vows, we all moved into an available three-bedroom apartment in the same Riverdale complex—with the dogs, which was nice. Ma Nay, that's what O and I were allowed to call Mrs. Naomi; she put on like she didn't like dogs, yet they slept at the foot of her bed. The apartment was packed and full of love. Exactly what I'd been missing. Family. Peewee even stopped accusing me of cheating on him. I can't explain what happened with him or why, for that matter...other than, he aged. Maturity. I guess we both matured, and I'm so grateful we came into ourselves together. We'll always have that.

I<small>F</small> M<small>ARCH</small> 27<small>TH</small> marked the day I decided to change, April 23rd of the same year ushered in a fresh start. I remember it like it was yesterday. Peewee and I barged into the apartment, excited to share some good news with Ma Nay. We were just getting back from shopping in Rockville center. The club needed fresh linen, nice dishes, and actual silverware. Peewee convinced Skee that it could use a woman's touch. He wasn't happy about any of the changes we were implementing and downright indignant over Peewee voicing our opinion and concerns. Skee sat behind a big oak desk in his private office at our shared establishment and nodded his head with his lips pursed, not saying much. Peewee and I had come to the conclusion that we wanted him out. Our dreams weren't cohesive.

"Maw!" Peewee yelled before I could get the door open. "Mawma!"

Ma Nay was in her usual spot—the kitchen on the phone. She held up a finger, asking for a moment. Her face was noticeably flushed.

"Your pain is not my emergency, Gladys..." She held her flip phone, talking to it like Ms. Gladys could see her. "I will not do this any longer; it's draining! We go through this every week." She stopped speaking and glanced up at us. We were frozen at the kitchen entry, surprised to hear the besties arguing. O and Junnie heard us coming in and joined us. "Gladys, I know, and yes I feel for you, but I will no longer be your emotional pin cushion. Sweetheart, it's not my responsibility." Ma Nay pinched the bridge of her nose and sat down in the chair she kept at the stove. She often expressed how much she disliked Gladys' man, Mr. Earl.

"I feel like you're holding me hostage in y'all relationship...and you ain't even married!" She paused again. I could hear Gladys yelling. Ms. Nay looked up and shook her head, asking us for another moment with her finger. "No, ah-ah, no ma'am...no more." She stood up, really irritated. "Bye, Gla——" Gladys must have cut her off because she stopped mid-sentence and winced. "Yeah, I said it...and meant it! Let's keep it one-hundred like the young folk say."

I heard Ms. Gladys clearly respond, "Well, I never!"

Ma Nay sorta chuckled. "And you never will, honey. Check this out." She adamantly pressed the end button on her tired flip phone. "Man, I wish I had a regular old house phone, so she could have felt that." She laughed, placing the cell on the countertop to check a boiling pot. "Greasy old heifer," she mumbled, still agitated. "I'll call her tomorrow."

Whatever happened, it couldn't break their friendship.

"Mawma," Peewee said again, coming from the shock of what we had just witnessed.

"Yes, love." She answered without looking up from her pot. "Ruthie, pass me the milk, please. I jumped to it, excited for her to hear our plans.

"Maw, ah ain't been...a-hun'nd wit-chew either," he continued, highlighting the term Ma Nay just used. "We been working with Skee Ball 'em——"

"Peewee!" Ma Nay sang, interrupting.

"Ah know, but before you get mad, all dat fitnah change." He walked further into the kitchen, placing a hand on her shoulder. Ma Nay glanced at me. She already knew about Skee. I'd told her during one of our one-on-one sessions while cooking. I nervously looked away and cleared my throat.

I really hated Skee and didn't trust him a bit. In the beginning, I tried to turn a blind eye to the dishonest things he was doing to us and our business; still, it was hard to do because they were so blunt. He was stealing our money and selling drugs.

"Ruthie and ah have decided to revamp Crescent City," Peewee continued, now addressing O and Junnie. "And dat means getting rid of Skee." O's mouth fell open. She had grown a rather suspicious closeness to Skee. She hung onto him like a groupie, and his intentions were obvious.

"Hold on, hold on, brother-in-law," she rolled her neck and twisted her hand. "How you gon' make these type decisions without including Junnie?" O knew Peewee always made the decisions. "I mean, he is a partnah." She tapped Junnie's leg to grab his attention. He was busy trying to sample the mashed potatoes Ma Nay was whisking. They were to accompany the bangin' pork chops filling the house with an aroma that was lit.

"Yeah...Peewee. Why you don't be asking me 'bout nothing?"

Peewee skinned up his face. "Niguh, since when ah ask you 'bout anything?" He sucked his teeth. "You straight trippin'! We fixin' to do things right and take back our business." He slightly pushed Junnie aside to address O directly. "Skee is making a strip club and crack house out of my dream. Ah want Mawma to come in on dis and start cooking for us." He added before O could say anything else.

"What?" Ma Nay asked, stopping her nervous work. She hated when any of us argued.

"Yeah, Maw. What Crescent City needs is a 24-hour presence. We got mad hours in de day to make money, ah don't understand why we limiting de establishment to weekends and Thursday, Friday nights? I'm talking money, O—not friendship." O sucked her teeth and rolled her eyes.

"Now, ah lak dat idea, Mawma." Junnie related, wrapping his mouth around a stolen chop.

"Boy!" Ma Nay squealed, wapping him with her whisk. "Get

outta here, pickin' over my food." Junnie laughed, running out of the kitchen from O's haunting eyes. "Ha, ha, hell!" Ma Nay continued, placing the food on the table in front of O. "Y'all make ya plates—you know I hate that pickin'." She sat at her stove seat, wiping sweat from her brow. "Now, Peewee, what you talkin 'bout, boy? I can't work in no kitchen, son. I just left one not so long ago."

"Ah know, but I'm talking 'bout you running de kitchen." He clarified piling a plate immediately.

"Nuh-uh!" O yelled, slapping his hand as he went for three chops. "You gon' leave some for everybody else?"

"What Peewee is saying is...," I added, making my plate before he and Junnie ate it all. "We would like you to consider managing the kitchen and guiding a professional cook in making your recipes. Good ole comfort food." I bit into my chop and did the happy dance. "Mmm, this is what I'm talking about. Your cooking is what Crescent City is missing." I nudged O's arm. "Come on, you know it's true." She was deep into her feelings and igging us.

"I'm not saying it's a bad idea. I'm just saying I don't like how Peewee be excluding his brother...and I don't know about getting rid of Skee either...I mean, is that even possible? I'm just saying." Feeling better about airing her grievance, she picked up a plate and started plating her and Junnie's food.

Ma Nay's face dropped in concern. "Lord, Peewee. I don't want y'all getting in no trouble with Skee Ball 'em——"

"Maw, don't let O sit here scaring you." He cut her off, giving O a dirty look. "Skee ain't put no money in dis business, only his name. I'm da boss, don't worry."

"Can I be there when you tell him that?" O laughed.

"You ain't said nuttin' but a thang, Mrs. Orpah Wiggins."

. . .

WE LEFT the apartment that night anticipating an eventful evening at the club. I vividly remember everyone's faces as we rode down the elevator. Junnie was hunched over with his head tucked into O's neck while rubbing her belly. She wore a wide, red-lipped smile, dishing trash talk toward Peewee about how he was fixing to get his butt kicked. Peewee laughed heartily, leaning against the elevator wall and holding me close against his body. I can still feel the warmth of his lips against my cheek as he paused to kiss me.

The elevator stopped. We got off on the lobby floor. Peewee's cell rang before we exited the building. It was Ma Nay asking that someone return. She had prepared a dinner plate for Skee, feeling it would help to soften the blow.

"Bae, can you please go back and get dis plate from Mawma?" Peewee asked, sucking his teeth. He didn't like the idea but was trying to appease her.

I rolled my eyes and turned, running back to catch the elevator before it left the lobby. As I stepped on, Junnie simultaneously opened the lobby door to exit the building. I pressed the button for the sixth floor and watched as the doors began to rigidly close behind me. Hearing an array of gunshots go off like fireworks in July, I quickly stuck my foot into the wedge of the closing doors. They reopened to a lobby fast filling with curious neighbors who had also heard the noise. My heart raced. My feet felt like bricks running toward the exit to ensure all was well. *Father God.*

My heart sank. The image of Peewee, Junnie, and O lying against the steps leading to the sidewalk with blood oozing from their limp bodies is an image I can never erase.

CHAPTER

SIXTEEN

NAOMI

O lived, but we lost the baby. Junnie died instantly. We kept a constant vigil by Peewee's bedside, but in my heart I knew it would be a matter of time before he slipped away. Peewee couldn't live without his Junnie. His fateful twin and hype man. It was only by God's holy presence, buffering the blow of the news, that I sustained.

My boys were murdered, gunned down like dogs in the street. That Skee Ball was no good, and I adamantly blamed him even though he carried on as if he was heartbroken. How does that saying go? The squeaky wheel makes the most noise. Skee was a loud, dirty, blood-thirsty Calliope thug. Deep in bed with sin. Pride was his necklace; he clothed himself with violence. From his callous heart came iniquity; his evil imagination had no limit. I spat on his crocodile tears. He and his goons set out to take over what Peewee made for the family. I couldn't even mourn their deaths properly until Skee was put under a cell.

God don't like ugly, that's what I always say. You can't live as Skee Ball did and expect a silver lining. I guess the same could be said about my boys—what goes around comes around. Their feet once hurried with deceit too. I don't know? All I knew was my babies were gone, and my spirit was crushed. My heart actually ached.

A few weeks after the boys' deaths, Skee was murdered. He was sitting behind his big oak desk at Crescent City and was shot point-blank by someone from his past.

Have you ever been weighed down by a plethora of problems so plentiful you felt dead and empty inside—nothing mattered. That's how it was for me. My boys were gone, and so was my desire to live. I had two daughters-in-law, two dogs, and a three-bedroom apartment with no savings or income other than Eli's Social Security to take care of all of them.

The girls and I floated around the house and each other, lifeless—like ghosts trying to hold on to the past. I didn't cook and can't recall us eating. When the bills started piling up, and O was fully healed from her wounds, the consensus was made unanimously amongst us—we were moving. We had nothing left for New York City to take. I spoke with Gladys, who was back in the Lower Ninth Ward on our beloved Delery Street in a newly built home. She insisted that we stay with her. Her grandbaby was grown and on her way out, and, praise God, Mr. Earl was gone too.

My grandmother used to say, "Never be afraid to trust an unknown future to an all-knowing God." My flesh and my heart may have failed me, but God was the strength of my life and portion forever. The girls and I began packing.

. . .

Iт's ridiculous the amount of stuff one can accumulate over time. After everything that happened, I found it easy to let go of it all. The boys and I came to New York City with nothing but the clothes on our backs and Uncle's car, and that's pretty much what I left with. If it couldn't fit in the trunk, we didn't need it. O was the only one who had a problem. She had so many clothes...so did Ruth, but the poor thing was so hurt she didn't care about any of it either. We packed what was fundamental, sold what we could, and gave away everything else. It would have been nice to be able to keep Peewee's car but we couldn't afford the car note, so it was repossessed. All we had was my dear sweet Eli's Social Security checks. That has to say something about honest work and integrity.

Ruth and I labored endlessly to tie off any loose ends. She found a new home for the dogs. They were old and pitiful but gained the love and stability they needed in Ruth's mom's best friend's home, Ms. Louis. My girl O was still trifling. She used her healing as an excuse not to help. Ruth and I spent our last few days in the city packing and saying goodbye to friends and family.

"What's this, Ma Nay?" Ruth asked while helping me break down my bed. It was the last piece of furniture to go. My friend, the social worker, Ms. Patrice, was taking it for her mom.

"Oh, my goodness!" I shouted, embarrassed that Ruth had found a more than half-empty bottle of peach brandy under the bed. "I'm done with that stuff," I said, defending my integrity and taking it from her. "I don't even know how old this is." I had bought it the week prior. There were about two shot glasses left. I opened the bottle and smelled it. In the back of my mind, BT Express was singing, "Do it, Do it—Do it til you satisfied."

"How 'bout a glass of liquid courage?" I asked, wanting company during my misery. Ruth sighed and plopped down on the floor. I joined her. We were dead tired. "One shot for me, one for you?"

"Nah, you go ahead," she waved me off before falling back into the plush cream-colored carpet that I took meticulous care of. "I'll get you a glass in a sec. I just need a little break." She added, stretching. "Ay, dios mio, my back."

"Don't bother," I said, taking a sip from the bottle. I was being a bad example. Lord knows that wasn't my intention. Ruth was doing well with weaning herself from her demons. I needed the crutch. My courage was drifting, and I completely understood how Eli must have felt all those years ago when we decided to move to New York. At my age, I should've been enjoying the fruits of my labor.

"Ahhh," I mouthed after a long swig and joined Ruth lying out on the floor. *Poor thing.* Her eyes were closed. "This time next week, we'll be in New Awlins."

"Mmhm," she groaned, falling asleep. I stretched over her to work a blanket off the edge of the mattress, then covered us with it. We passed out right there on the floor.

CHAPTER

SEVENTEEN

RUTH

"I'm leaving tomorrow, Abuela," I explained again to my grandmother. She was trying to understand what was happening. For some reason, she was the only person holding me to the city.

Abuela had gotten old. She wasn't sickly; she was too ornery for that. However, she wasn't as sharp as she used to be. Her movements were slow, and her thoughts and words, yet intentional and deliberate, were dragged out.

"You and your mother have never taken my advice." She reached by her side and pulled out a wand lighter tucked between the pillows on the sofa where we sat. She lit yet another candle. There were already many burning around the apartment—which was another concern of mine.

"This woman you're with," she continued while smothering bundled sage. "In the time you've been together, she put a lot of wisdom in you." She fanned the smoke my way; I winced, waving it back toward her. Abuela's eyes searched her small, cluttered apartment as though reflecting over her life. "Ay, no sé," she said, surprising me by taking my hand into hers. Deep wrinkles had formed creases into her skin. I could feel the grooves with my thumb, yet her palms were soft and smooth. "Ruthie, we have never seen eye to eye." She patted my hand. "You should go. I have nothing more to give you." My eyes started to tear. Deep inside, I wanted Abuela to want and need me. However, oddly enough, I felt relieved to hear her say go.

"Abuela..." I tried to speak but croaked on my words. "If you need me, I will stay."

She smiled, looking around the room again. "Go get the picture of your grandfather," she ordered, waving me off.

Here we go. I followed her orders, bottling up my emotions. *Every time we take a step forward, we take two steps back.*

"Aquí." I roughly handed Abuela the picture and sat on the coffee table to face her. I wanted to see her eyes when she fed me her B.S. for the last time.

"Your grandfather was a handsome man." She ran an arthritis-curved finger along the face of the man behind the glass. "All the young women in our village wanted to marry him." She added after a slight pause. That piece of information was new and more than I'd ever heard. "But! He chose one girl to marry...and that girl was not me."

My mouth fell open.

"I've never needed anyone, Ruthie. You should go be with your mother-in-law." She opened the back of the frame and removed a hidden smaller wallet-size picture that was frayed and yellowing with age. "This is your real grandfather." She gently kissed the picture before placing it in my hand, smiling with pride. "Qué guapo está...qué pollo!" which is Spanish slang for hot stuff! Equivalent to calling someone a fox.

He looked like Mami, and I began to cry. She would have loved to see that picture.

"For whatever reason," Abuela continued, shrugging her shoulders, "no sé...he didn't choose to marry me." She took the picture and smiled down at the man again. "I took what he gave me...and lived for us." She looked down at the opened frame with the picture of the military man. "That is not your abuelo. He's just a man. Un sueño. A dream that kept me going. A lie to give you heritage...and dig-ni-ty." She patted my hand again. "Now, you go make your own family. Find a good husband...one who will provide with his hands and honor. Have many babies."

Besides the church experience, I had never felt more alive than in that moment. I left Abuela's apartment feeling lighter. She wasn't perfect, but she tried to make life perfect for us. She felt she failed with Mami. In me, she saw a fighting chance. So, Abuela freed me from the lies she told and gave me her blessings.

"God alone is the only one who can fulfill the desires of the heart. Go in peace, Muñequita. Dios te bendiga"

CHAPTER
EIGHTEEN

NAOMI

With my two daughters-in-law, I left the place where I had been living and set out on the road that would take us back to the Lower Ninth Ward in New Orleans. Back to my beginning. That's the part I had conflict with. Was I dragging two young women at the prime of their lives into my dying situation, further into my misery and misfortune? With the pressure of anxiety upon me, I pulled over after only driving a few blocks.

"What's wrong," O asked. She was sitting by me and up next to drive. We both wore glasses and had trouble seeing at night. Ruth was the designated night driver.

"Did we forget something," Ruth questioned, trying to get comfortable amongst O's stuff—forcefully packed into the back seat of Uncle's old Caddie. It had seen better days.

I shut the car off and turned in my seat with a stern look

etched upon my face. "Y'all go back...both of you, to your own families." I quickly said before taking it back. There was nothing in the Ninth Ward for them. No jobs. No young men. No homes. Gladys had told me that the community was still pretty much vacant, and that people were slowly moving back.

Delery Street was our home; Gladys and I. There was an old-fashioned sense of community there that today's youth know nothing about. Folks lived by bedrock values like respecting their elders and praising the Lord.

"May God show you kindness, girls, because only He knows how kind y'all have been to me and my sons." I took each of their hands. Our eyes were starting to well with water. "I pray that He grants each of you satisfaction in the home of another husband." I kissed their foreheads as we huddled in and cried aloud.

"No, Ma Nay, we're going with you."

I shook my head, thinking of how kind they'd been to me despite our rough start. "Please stay, girls. Why would you come with me?" I released myself from their embrace and quickly wiped my tears, attempting to now be stern. "I can't give y'all more sons to marry. Go home. I'm too old to provide for your needs. I'll only be a burden. Even if I thought there was still hope—would you remain unmarried for my sake? No, that's nonsense." This time, I shook my head with more authority. "Trust me. It's more bitter for me than for you." I turned back in my seat, embarrassed. "The Lord's hand has turned against me."

"No, don't say that," Ruth cried, patting my shoulder, but O kissed me goodbye.

"She's right, Ruth," she insisted, acknowledging my disclaimer and turning in her seat to face Ruth head-on. "We don't know anything about New Orleans...what the heck are we gonna do out there?"

But Ruth clung to me.

93

"Look," I said, attempting to convince her otherwise. "Your bestie is staying with her family...and everything else familiar." Without turning my head, I rubbed her arms wrapped around my shoulders. "Go with her."

"Don't ask me to leave or turn my back on you," Ruth replied. She vanished her tears and focused on O. "Listen...I get it. You have a large crazy family to go back to." She chuckled. "Y'all got each other, and that's great! I have no one...but you and Ma Nay—"

"Don't say that! You know my peeps is ya peeps. We can figure this out together," O interrupted, grasping Ruth's hands and practically pleading with her.

I was breaking up a friendship and felt small in my seat. I needed a cigarette but had gotten used to not smoking in front of O. Instead, I stared at the neighborhood that had been my home for ten years and attempted to divert my craving and give the girls space to talk. Nothing in New York City felt irreplaceable. There was no way I was staying. Then Ruth said.

"O, you know I love you; you my girl for life. I need to go with Ma Nay. I can't leave her. I owe this to Peewee."

"Whoo, whoo! No, you don't!" I interrupted, coming from my thoughts. "The Word says to owe no one anything except to love each other. No one owes my boys or me NOTHING!" I rocked in my seat making my statement clear, then turned my face sideways to her. "You have given ya self in love, Ruth. Peewee would not want you to give up ya life for him...well?" We all chuckled. "Maybe he would, but I don't. I don't want that for you, Ruthie."

Ruth's face became stern, and from the cramped backseat she zoomed in on my eyes through the rearview mirror. "Listen, Ma Nay, wherever you go, I'm going, and where you stay, I'll stay." I turned to face her because I felt the presence of a fourth party in the car. Ruth's response wasn't even on the level of her understanding...it was higher. She was speaking what the Holy Spirit conveyed. "Your family will be my family, and ya God my God. So help me; where you die, I'll die, and I'll be buried right there next to you," she insisted without batting an eye. Ruth held up her right hand as though taking an oath. "May God deal with me alone if anything but death separates us!"

There was nothing to say, not after that. O and I locked our jaws and didn't utter a word. Ruth was determined to go, so we stopped urging her.

Even the best of friends must part.

We helped O unload her stuff and called an Uber Black.

ALTHOUGH I WAS FRIGHTENED, I abandoned control of my life to His will and walked by faith into the next phase. I turned to the oldies station on the radio and reclined my seat. Bloodstone was singing, giving me the "Natural High" I needed as Ruthie Mercedes Wiggins zoomed down that same twisting road toward New Orleans.

CHAPTER
NINETEEN

RUTH

It's funny how you get to know a person when you're stuck in a car with them for hours. There was a lot that was familiar about Ma Nay. She wasn't always a bible thumper. She wasn't always a mother. She was a girl from the projects of Chicago. A girl who knew the harsh realities of life and overcame so many battles. She spoke with experience, not to belittle me but to educate me. As we traveled the open highway, she opened her heart and allowed me to see the soul of a real woman. I envied her and prayed to be half the woman she was.

My heart was broken, but I could only imagine how it must have felt to be a mother losing not one but both of her children...a grandchild and a husband? How does a person pick up the pieces and continue life as it comes? I tried to feel sorry for myself, but Ma Nay appeared to be a rock. I found myself wanting to be strong for her.

As I drove through the starry-lit night surrounding unknown territory, I reflected over my life and time with Peewee. There was a lot we did wrong but also a lot we did right. We lived. We enjoyed life. We conquered fears. We loved each other in our own way.

"Is this a private reverie, or can an old lady join you?" Ma Nay asked, waking from a nap. We were in Tennessee and heading toward our first and hopefully only overnight stop.

"Just thinking," I answered, coming from deep thought. I was playing an old Usher CD that Peewee bought me years ago. I loved Usher and Peewee knew he partly owed him credit for our hook-up. If he didn't look like him, he would've never been "My Boo". I turned the track down.

"How much further?" Ma Nay asked, rubbing her neck. "I need a bed and a shower badly."

"I know that's right...me too. In about forty minutes, we'll be in Mohawk, Tennessee."

She nodded her head in approval of our schedule. "This time tomorrow, we'll be there and in our new bed."

"Yup," I said dryly. I was excited but nervous. Peewee and I traveled once to New Orleans to get Skee. He didn't fly and had his driver's license revoked. I couldn't say much about The Crescent City then; we were in the hood. I was from the hood. If you've seen one, you've seen them all.

"You sure you gonna be okay with all this? I'm feeling kinda nervous about you giving up so much."

I laughed and quickly glanced at her, "Yeah, right, like I had so much going for me."

Ma Nay looked concerned. She probably fell asleep thinking about our conversations and woke up worried. "I just don't want you to resent me."

I removed a hand from the wheel and patted hers. "You ain't holding no gun to my head, Ma. I'm doing this by my own...kahunas." I sort of chuckled, returning my hand.

"Ruth, you're only in the autumn of your life; there's seasons ahead. I don't want you sitting around growing old with Gladys and me."

I really laughed. "Trust and believe, I don't plan on sitting around y'all doing nothing. I got plans." I lied, having not a clue besides finding work. I'll admit, at that moment my mind briefly wandered toward my old ways of thinking. You know—find a playah and let him take care of you. But I didn't want that for myself. I intended on standing on my own two feet. Jokingly, I said differently. Kinda feeling Ma Nay's opinions out.

"If all else fails, I can find us some boo thangs." I glanced to see her expression.

She threw an askance look my way before her belly rolled with thunderous laughter. "Gurl! The devil is a liar." she proclaimed, wiping tears from her eyes. "I be darned...as old as I am?"

I laughed with her. It was good to see Ma Nay laughing. "You don't ever think about hooking up? Getting a lil piece?" I asked, now curious about her needs. She was a woman first.

"Chile, please! You and that O got some smart mouths...but y'all as honest as they come. That's right..." She pulled out a cigarette. "...don't hold back ya feelings or thoughts. Put 'em out there...I like that 'bout y'all." She cracked the window. "You think I don't understand." She blew her smoke out. "I used to have perky little titties once upon a time too, you know. That don't make you special. Using your body to get what you want. I been there...and I tried it with Eli."

"Whaaat!" My mouth fell open as I glanced her way. "I thought you were like Mother Teresa or somebody." We laughed together. "Do tell." I needed to feel like I wasn't alone in my behavior. "Open the closet door." I motioned with my hand for her to continue talking, "Let's see what the heck flies out!"

Ma Nay's laughter became nervous giggles. "No, I'm far from nunhood, baby girl." She took a long puff of the cigarette which she had supposedly quit smoking, then allowed it to float out the window and down the highway along with her smoke. "Why do you think I'm so hard, huh? It's not all because my man went and died on me...left me with two boys to raise on my own. Nah! And it ain't because them boys gave me such hell I liked to run out on 'em. No, ma'am." The laughter was gone, and she was more sincere. "I had a life before I came to be a wife and mama. A hard one too. What's that Sophia said in that movie—girl chile ain't safe. I didn't meet Elimelech Wiggins and instantly fell in love...the man had a darn good job with benefits, and I needed out. You let that sink in." She leaned into the pause she presented as I thought about how lucky she was to find such love in spite of herself.

I guess God does work in mysterious ways.

"Stumbling upon a good man like Eli was a blessing—those type batteries aren't included when you know life as hard as you and I do. Me and Eli's meeting was nothing but God. Eli found me —although I thought I worked him over. He saw something that I hadn't seen in myself...and he lived the rest of his life confirming it." She reached over and brushed my thigh. "You're a gorgeous young woman, Ruth. Take it from an old lady. There will always be someone prettier working ya turf. It's time you believe in your-self, for you. Like I been telling you, beauty is fleeting. Can you picture me as a young hot fox?" She laughed, playfully running her hands down the curves of her body as I tried to imagine her young and fine.

Ma Nay wasn't a bad-looking woman. She took care of her skin and hair and dressed neatly. I could see an older man falling for her if she put herself back out there. Yet, I understood what she was trying to say, and I wanted that confidence in myself.

"A beautiful woman who lacks discretion is like a gold ring in a pig's snout," she added, using her quotes again. "That type of behavior ain't for you." She insisted, as though knowing my initial thoughts. "You are not meant to be that type of woman. You're a lady."

I chuckled, "I ain't never been called no lady."

"Well, shame on Peewee, because you are. If a man can't see that and treat you as such...he ain't worth your time or energy."

"How do you know what they think of you?"

She thought for a moment, then smiled and said, "It's all in how he treats you. How he makes you feel. Opening doors. Giving you flowers and taking you on trips. Those things are nice...but there's so much more. When a man loves you, he respects and appreciates you...to the point where he almost treats you better than he treats himself. He thinks of you first. Your well-being, your reputation, your feelings. He looks to please you and makes sacrifices. You find yourself feeling free to be yourself around him. You discover you're a woman in his presence. He doesn't simply love you because you're pretty...or good in the sack. All of that is self-gratifying—for his bragging rights. A good woman makes a man look good. He walks with dignity and integrity. Him, and their children, shall rise up and call her blessed. Ruth, darlin', what you was doing was getting in ya own way. I loved my sons, but don't let your heart be drawn to that which is evil. I pray for the sake of all ya souls that you changed."

Ma Nay had my head spinning. The darkened sky surrounding the highway became the canvas for my wandering thoughts. *Buggy and Peewee.* My only love interests. *Did I love them...or was our love built on what they gave me?* The only thing I knew for sure was that my hope was now in Jesus. What He had for me, I wanted.

In mid-thought, the check engine light quickly flashed before all power in the car shut down. Instantly, everything slowed.

CHAPTER
TWENTY

NAOMI

If it wasn't for bad luck, we wouldn't have had any luck at all.

The engine in Uncle's car gave out. I hadn't done my part in preserving its lifetime. I couldn't afford it. Something else always took precedence over its care.

Ruth and I found ourselves alone, two women of color on the side of a dark Tennessee road. I immediately went into prayer mode as we walked, trying to catch a signal to make a call to AAA. Thank Goodness Peewee had a yearly membership. That he took care of. He loved his cars and traveling.

"God is our refuge and strength, an ever-present help in trouble..." I spoke out loud with authority, claiming each word as we ventured on in total darkness. Not a street light to be seen. Ruth fidgeted with her phone.

"CRAP! No, signal," she stated for the fifth time, frustrated and sucking her teeth while shining the cell's flashlight on our path.

"We will not fear...," I reminded her. We couldn't. Though shadows lurked around us with strange sounds coming from every direction. Fear wasn't an option. We had resolutely headed out, making a fresh start and literally leaving everything and everyone behind. So, we marched arm in arm until the bars on the cell phone appeared. "We will not fear!"

After walking a mile up the road, we were able to reach AAA. We waited over two hours for them, locked away in a stalled car surrounded by the mysteries of the night.

That evening, after we were rescued, we squeezed together, snug like bugs in a rug in a double-sized bed at a suspicious-looking motel, etched into a corner on a dead-end road of a small walk through town. It was rather Bates Motel-ish. We cramped in together, trembling until we fell asleep.

The next day we were told that the engine was gone and not worth the fix. The car was in such bad condition. Ruth and I, with our red scratchy, dry eyes from lack of sleep, were pointed to a local Greyhound station. With two hundred dollars left between us, we purchased two tickets at fifty dollars each and proceeded with our trip, refusing to give up. Unfortunately, we had to leave even more of our things behind. I had bed and bath linen neatly packed into a large construction bag, not allowed on the bus. Ruth had an open box full of her mom's belongings. She squeezed what she could into our already overstuffed luggage, a picture album, some clothes, and her mom's jewelry, then took a picture of whatever was left and bravely tossed the box in the garbage. I knew it was hard for her to do. All my memories and treasures were washed away by Katrina. Every now and then, I think about them, but ultimately life proceeds without possessions.

. . .

EVERYTHING about the bus was drab. Not only was it faded in dingy tones, but the passengers were washed out, beaten up, and overdone. Ruth and I were on the right bus. A drab bus going back to the past instead of the future. Go backward. That's exactly what we're told not to do.

"Do you think all this a sign?" I leaned against Ruth's arm and whispered her way. I could be stubborn at times, and at that point in my life I couldn't afford to miss His will for me. I felt like something was against us.

"I don't," Ruth answered, with her head comfortably rested against the dingy headrest. My OCD made it hard for me to get comfortable. That bus needed a good bleaching. "You think too much," she continued, opening her eyes to address me directly. "Don't you always say you can't trust God and worry?" She raised her eyebrows knowingly. "Can any one of us by worrying add a single hour to our life...is that how it goes?"

"I know. I know. But doesn't it seem odd that all this is happening to us now? Maybe, He's trying to turn us back."

"Or maybe He's trying to get us to trust Him alone." She closed her eyes again.

How can she sleep at a time like this? I gazed out of the window nearest me. *She could be right. My little grasshopper is growing up.* I was proud of Ruth for taking the stance of faith all by herself in spite of my withering emotions. *Lord, I hope she's right.* I prayed, watching the telephone lines float from pole to pole down the wide country road. Tears ran down my face. I was scared. Scared of failure. Scared of the unknown. Scared of misleading Ruth.

Father, I know you can do all things...but it seems like I call you... but you never answer. When I pray, you pay no attention. Don't you care about me anymore? If you are silent...I might as well give up and die.

I fell asleep in wonder, and, in that quiet moment, heard a voice I hadn't heard in a long time. It was loud yet quiet...it was audible yet from the depth of my being.

"Never will I leave you nor forsake you. My grace is sufficient. My power is made perfect in your weakness."

PART: TWO

So Naomi returned from Moab accompanied by Ruth the Moabite, her daughter-in-law, arriving in Bethlehem as the barley harvest was beginning.
Ruth 1:22

CHAPTER
TWENTY-ONE

BOAZ

When Pa died, both Ma and I went into shock. It was so surreal that in my mind, I envisioned my father had been abducted and would return in the future. I used to sit in the yard at night and gaze up at the stars wishing and praying that he would return. There was some sort of mistake, a miscount of souls needed in heaven that week.

Like myself, more than anything, Ma wanted to believe that there had been a mistake too. Pa would be revived at the hospital, and we would continue our lives, 'happily ever Abrams'. But that wasn't the case. Pa had tragically died on the call of duty. Ironically—probably as he would have preferred.

Time brought healing; Ma threw herself into her businesses. Her small organic skincare empire tripled in revenue. I worked our farmland. Three thousand acres of God's land, free and clear. Twenty percent organic fruits and vegetables, eighty percent feed grain. The tedious labor occupied my mind. I didn't want to exist in day-to-day living anymore. I'd rather hang out in the wonders of germination. It was the closest to God that I could understand. He took away to bring forth, to take again. The circle of life.

After our first lucrative harvest, Ma reopened the restaurant inherited on the property. She hated to see good food go to waste, especially fresh food. What we didn't sell, she used from farm to table. Being miles away from the city limit, it took a minute and a lot of vision, support, and craftiness for the restaurant to build back up revenue. An organic restaurant along the route to debauchery wasn't necessarily ideal.

Once we got things rolling with the local supermarkets and farmers' markets in town, we were on our way. Ma became known as the pie lady. Her various fresh pies, jams, and popular lemon and lavender hemp shortbread cookies were incorporated into the markets to lure people to the brick-and-mortar location. Before we knew it, the restaurant quickly became a local and tourist favorite. Ma had recipes from her childhood committed to memory. They were true down-home treasures intermixed with the edginess of her New York City past. Like the Smokin' Smoked Brisket with Dope Sauce and Get Busy Wit It baked beans. Ma's hands had an anointing over them. Whatever she touched turned to gold. She put a lot of love into her food and work. The restaurant was named Gettin' Fresh Café. *Bronx woman, by way of the Bayou, gets fresh in the garden,* is what the front page article of a local agricultural newspaper read.

People became Ma's joy, and they adored and adopted Ms. Pie, the pie lady, as their own. I sort of disappeared behind the business end of things and behind the tall shafts of grain that primarily funded the farm, keeping a watchful eye over her. We were all we had, besides Paw-Paw and Tante Tita, who popped in every now and then to check in on us.

Everyone was worried about my well-being and relationship status. Ma said I was ornery and treated her as though she was a child. I viewed her as my responsibility. She called me 'old man', but I'd take it if that meant I kept her safe.

After Pa died, the gnawing pain never rested. The churning inside of me never stopped. My whole heart was afflicted. From the sole of my feet to the top of my head, there was no soundness —only wounds and welts. I carried the loss like an amputation. My anger was easily aroused because I was mad at God. It took a lot of convincing to get on speaking terms with Him again—even greater convincing to profess His name in praise. But I was my father's and Paw-Paw's child, a preacher at heart. I knew from whence my blessings came. The sourness I felt from losing Pa was hard to erase. The public and private person were affected and at war within me, but my faith remained.

I was twenty-nine years old, single with no kids nor prospects. Talk about being stuck in your ways. I was stubborn to the T—it was mostly control issues. I had to protect and provide. The only way for me to do that was to maintain our environment. Of course, I was attracted to women. Besides being a successful farmer and businessman, I was an assistant pastor at our family church. The only women who I encountered and passed my level of standards regarding an appropriate mate were single mothers. Nothing against single moms. Still, they are not the type of women to experiment with. I was the one date king. I sat and compared every woman with and to my mother. How would they communicate? Would they want to involve her in our lives? Would they help or hinder our businesses? Those thoughts kept me on the farm and hiding amongst the grain.

. . .

"Son, your father was a good man. What he did, he did naturally." Every now and again, Ma felt the need to redirect me.

"Ah know, Ma." We were in the garden picking field peas. Part of the farm was devoted to CSA, community-supported agriculture. We ran a very streamlined and efficient operation. We were not alone. The garden and orchard were full of idealistic people bagging groceries for themselves, planting, and helping us to harvest for the markets and pantry programs.

"I just want you to hear me," Ma continued, "I'm worried about you." She stopped picking and rested troubled eyes on my face.

"Ma, I'm okay," I smiled, pointing at my mouth with a pea pod, "you de one worried."

"I feel like you're trying to live up to a ghost. Trying to be someone who was living the life meant for them." I grew quiet. Talking about Pa hurt. "Your dad was a soldier. He was created for that." She got back into her groove of picking while smiling and reminiscing over her time spent with Pa. "I didn't want him to be, but he was. He was the type of person who would give his life for others...and he knew every day that there was a risk of him not seeing us again." She sort of chuckled. "He was like that since we were kids, always the hero."

"Someone's gotta do it, right?" I turned my back to her and started another row, wishing Pa hadn't been the one.

"It was his calling," Ma continued. "His place in this world. Just like we need doctors to heal, or people who invent things and build...or farmers..." She nudged my back. "Those who harvest and care for the land. Sal knew his place, and he lived every day thankful for his blessings. I'm blessed and honored to have loved such a man as long as I did." She turned me around. "So, don't you go feeling sorry for me...ya pa...or yourself. Instead, find out who you are in this world. Give that all you got...not this!" She stretched her arms, turning between the rows of the purple hull field peas we were picking. They were on the menu that night. I can almost taste them now with cornbread.

Ma tucked my stray hairs behind my ears. I was letting it grow out like Pa's, yet mine was curly like hers. "I see a lot of him in you. Look how you've given up on a life for yourself just to protect me." She palmed my face, forcing me to look her way. "Ya mama's gonna be fine. You don't have to replace ya dad, old man. Don't you know that I delight in your success and achievements?" My eyes slightly watered, and I turned away, lowering the Stetson on my head. "Don't let me hold you back from love, Shadow," she went on without remorse. "I'm waiting patiently for grandbabies. Son, when you gon' give me some?" She wrapped her short arms around my waist, shaking me up a little.

I laughed, removing my hat and wiping my arm across my sweaty brow. The sun was directly over us. Ma nudged me before getting back to her work. She knew there was no winning with me and that topic. I winced, looking up at the midday sun, thinking of her question but mostly of tomorrow's work. It was harvest time. The next few months would be consumed with grain. Harvesting grain. Bagging grain. Selling grain. Then, there was the harvest festival, which always fell before Paw-Paw's birthday. There was a lot to do and plan. A large part of me wished I had a wife and confidant to share my thoughts, fears, and life with.

"Ma," I said, standing between the rows of peas, caught between work and living.

"Yes, love." She answered, busy picking; she had to stop soon to manage the lunch rush.

"How you know when a woman loves you...how you know she de one?" I asked as though there were many contenders.

Ma stopped and picked up her full bucket, thinking as she walked over. "When a woman loves you..." she said, handing me the bucket, "she can't get enough of you." She wiped her brow with the handkerchief hanging from her overall pocket. The initials S.A. were embroidered on it. "She finds herself wanting to be near you...because it's easy to be in your presence." She smiled like she used to with Pa. "It's like she's breathing for the first time because she's safe to be herself." Her eyes wandered back from memories and rested on mine. "You make her feel like a woman...and you'll innately know that she's the one because the man in you will rise to the occasion of caring for her as your wife." She smiled and patted my face. "You'll just know. Don't limit love to your perspective and understanding of life. It's a mystery worth exploring...just like this farm." She spread her arms again, turning playfully as she walked away, smiling. "Stop thinking that you should live an error-free life, old man..." she yelled, turning again to add, "that's symptomatic of pride."

TWENTY-TWO

RUTH

We arrived in town looking and smelling like vagabonds; dirty, tired, and scruffy. There was a long layover and bus change in Mississippi. My Louis Vuitton luggage set did not make the change, and I arrived in New Orleans empty-handed. Ma Nay said she felt in her spirit that would happen. "Someone made off with them bags," she said. I was distraught. Everything I had and treasured was in them—except my wedding ring, which was on a chain around my neck, and what I managed to squeeze into Ma Nay's luggage. My mother's picture album and her favorite house gown were all I had of my past.

Mad as hell, I had to suck it all up because my companion was visibly fixing to have a meltdown. Not another thing could go wrong. The rock she resembled when we left New York City turned into gravel. I filed a claim report at the bus station, and we caught an Uber to Delery Street.

Ms. Gladys met us from her front porch seat. She was a short, overweight woman with legs that bent into parentheses under her. Unable to quickly stand, she excitedly waved from her seat as we drove onto the driveway.

"Hey, y'all! Hey!" She shouted, trying to reach for a walker resting against the railing across from her. "Destiny! Destiny, get out here, gal!" She yelled toward the screen door of the tiny black and white builder-grade home. "How de heck I'm sposed to get my walker all de way o'va der?" She questioned, annoyed at the young girl who appeared in the doorway. It was apparent why Ma Nay was needed. Ms. Glady rolled her eyes at Destiny and grabbed her arm for support as she addressed her old friend. "Oh, my goodness. Is that really you, Naomi?" She struggled to stand. Destiny was no help. All she offered was a limp arm for assistance. She was more interested in the Uber driver.

"Don't call me, Naomi," Ma Nay responded, getting out of the car. "Call me bitter; because God has dealt very bitterly with me." She slowly shuffled up the driveway, her feet and legs swollen from hours of travel. "Jehovah has brought me home empty, Gladys." She began to cry. "He's testified against me, girl." Once she reached her friend's outstretched arm, they embraced and wept aloud. Years of tears.

The Uber driver left, and I stood alone in the driveway, surrounded by Ma Nay's bags.

Noticing another one of Destiny's neglects, Ms. Gladys quickly wiped away her tears and yelled, "Shut de damn screen door, dummy! You letting flies in de house!" She shook her head, looking at Ma Nay like, *see what I have to deal with.* They took each other's arms, and both being overweight, daringly plopped down on a wicker loveseat together, laughing.

So, this is New Orleans? I picked up a bag and started for the stairs.

TWENTY-THREE

NAOMI

Moving back to the Ninth Ward was hard—not at all as I envisioned. I lost momentum with each downward mile we traveled. I wanted to be strong for Ruth. I wanted to be sure of the decision we were making. But everything in me screamed, *what the...*! We didn't have a real plan besides helping Gladys, who needed assistance getting around.

Gladys had always been overweight, but she told me she gained extreme weight after Katrina—binge eating from depression. She could hardly stand. I completely understood; food was comforting for me as well. I had lost and gained weight over the years too.

Coming back into town, I instantly picked up Gladys' anxieties. Our old neighborhood was pretty much vacant. Scattered homes stood like old reflections against empty lots. There was a hole where my house once stood, which pretty much summed up my feelings. An empty hole. How could I ask Ruth to remain there with me? It was like living amongst the dead; we were trying to escape death and dying. For the time being, Gladys was familiar.

I washed away my sorrows playing Pitty-Pat and gossiping with my old friend while Ruth wandered like a zombie amongst us. Destiny, Gladys' granddaughter, was so glad to see us that she moved the day we arrived. I couldn't blame her. Her youth was waiting. Just as Ruth's was. What would she do in the weed-infested rural community? There weren't many young folks there, to begin with. The population only aged, and when the kids moved, they never returned. I was scared for Ruth.

"Are you using this time to heal, or are you just trying not to think about things?" I asked her one day. She did a lot of walking when she wasn't running errands for Gladys and me.

"Honestly, I don't know," Ruth responded.

We were drinking pops on the porch. Gladys was at a doctor's appointment that she didn't want anyone to know about. She was being very secretive about her health, which worried me too. It couldn't have been good news.

"I feel like a stranger here," Ruth continued. She was sitting on the steps barefoot in an orange sun dress we picked up at Target. It was a week later, and her things still hadn't arrived. We deemed them gone forever.

Ruth had nothing. She and Peewee put all they had into the club—and what they made in profit was taken away in bills and rent before the establishment closed altogether. More than ever, I saw myself in her.

"I'm sorry, Ruth." I lowered my head, massaging the bridge of my nose. "This was a bad idea."

Ruth turned to face me. We were watching yet another older couple move onto the block. "I didn't say I was unhappy. I just gotta find where I fit in." She had to be lying for my sake; she obviously was unhappy. I was. However, I could've been content if she was happier—established at least. "I been looking for work...nothing so far." She turned back to the movers though watching them was getting boring. "I'm worried about you, Ma." She rested her pop bottle on the steps. "You not the same." She turned back toward me. "Are you healed or just trying to forget everything?" She asked, recycling my concerns. A tear came to my eye because I knew I wasn't completely healed from the pain. I wore it like a full-length winter coat in the beautiful Louisiana weather.

I sighed. "I'm trying." The tears fell. Ruth looked away from me.

"I'm gonna find a job tomorrow," she responded, always thinking money was the answer. It wasn't. Wealth is worthless in the day of wrath. "Maybe I've been aiming too high," she continued, "I wanna be able to use my degrees, you know?" I nodded, remembering all the time she put into her schooling in memory of her mom. "I'm afraid I'm overqualified here. Maybe I should aim lower for right now."

I knew my face read my concerns. I wanted the best for Ruth —my thoughts leaned towards her happiness. "Don't worry— this too shall pass."

She leaned over and stretched her slender arm across the porch, patting my foot. "I think you're awesome," she said, bringing a smile to my face despite our despair.

"You ain't slight either, kiddo."

CHAPTER
TWENTY-FOUR

RUTH

The next day I set out to recover my life and put Ma Nay's mind to ease. I'd been eyeing a club about an hour and fifteen minutes away from the house on foot. It was sitting in the middle of an empty block as though the sole survivor of the area's devastation. Although the block was empty, there was a lot of activity in the building. It was a strip club and from what I could see, a booming business.

My first thought was, *I know I have the talent to help run a place like this.* My second thought was, *...or I can dance and make some quick money.* Even though I was dressed like someone's mother, I was still hot. I just needed the motivation to walk in and inquire. I'd never considered doing anything like that, at least not publicly. In the past, I played men for money and did things I regretted. At that moment, the major issue jabbing at my spirit like a splinter stuck in my foot was that I knew better. That annoyed me. I had grown a conscience. Morals. My faith said, ***your body is a temple.***

I stood in front of the club early that Thursday morning before they opened ping-ponging my thoughts before making a final decision. I knew a lot of girls who danced in the city, including O —before we met the guys. From the looks of her Instagram page, she was dabbling in it again. The outfits she posted in didn't look like a day at the office attire, and she had become hard to reach. From what I recalled, O loved dancing. She loved all the attention. That was O. I don't want to call my friend trifling but...she was at times.

Then there was Ma Nay. Her well-being was my main concern. I needed to step up my game on her behalf, yet I knew how she would feel about me stripping. *I could lie about it—tell her I got a job elsewhere.* Seeing me move forward would encourage Ma Nay to regain her life. Somehow I needed to give her back what I felt she'd lost—-her sense of being. Her depression ran deeper than losing loved ones. She lost herself. In that way, we both were alike. I needed to feel important again too.

I knew that the Lord was working on my behalf. I could feel it in His stripping away of everything I thought I wanted and needed—from my clothes to the image I had of myself. However, calamity was hungry within me too—you know how it is when you want to change your life and start doing what's right? In the back of your head, the old you is speaking. My past was saying, *get that paper! It'll make it all better.* What I was really doing was trying to move God along in the process of restoration.

"Excuse me, ma'am." I heard from behind. I quickly turned but saw no one in particular seeking my attention. There was a group of men lined up waiting to board some sort of a shuttle bus.

"Excuse me, ma'am." I heard the voice say again. The workers parted, allowing the driver to direct his question toward me. "Are you coming?" He smiled wide, and I promise you, I can honestly say that I felt that smile all the way down in my toes. I must have looked confused because this man, looking like a chocolate-covered blessing, repeated himself with another Colgate smile. "Are you coming?"

They say that behind every smile is an untold story. Quickly, I turned from his beauty. The last thing I needed was a distraction or drama. *He can't be talking to me. He must have mistaken me for someone else.*

"We have work," he reiterated, and I turned back, intrigued. Only God could pull me away from making the biggest mistake of my life by gift wrapping possibility and dangling it in front of my eyes. The entire incident was shrouded in mystery, but there was a swirl of need that led me to get on that bus.

CHAPTER
TWENTY-FIVE

BOAZ

S he was a vision in white. Never had I seen someone so radiant in the glow of the Lord. She stood out like a 3D image against the typical morning happenings. Twice a week, I parked in front of Blitz Dance Hall, loading workers for the farm. Twice a week, I zoned out in routine ritual, trying to make eye contact with a smile.

"God be with you," I said to each person with a nod as Mr. Ralph used to do when he drove the shuttle. He was now a foreman.

The workers answered, "God bless you, Mr. Bo."

Ma insisted that I start making more personal connections. However, I knew she was hoping I'd meet a young lady. "You're a handsome guy," she said. "Why are you hiding that smile? Don't merely be a hearer of the Word, Shadow, be a doer—authentically. Let your light shine."

I'll admit it, I was an intense fella. It wasn't my intention—I guess I was always in my head. That morning unexpectedly and just like that, my authentic smile resurfaced. I saw an angel standing in front of the strip club with her fingers pushed back into her hair like she was stressing over something. Every ounce of my being shouted, **call out to her**.

"Excuse me, ma'am," I heard myself say before my brain could stop me.

Searching for my voice, the vision turned as though in a slow-motion reel—hair flowing, skin flawless, birds chirping. Her beauty was even greater than the radiant glow. The workers were loading the van, and she didn't see me, but I could see her. That's when the smile that read boyish, curious, and awestruck spread across my face. I motioned for the guys to move aside.

"Excuse me, ma'am," I repeated, and our eyes connected. "Are you coming?"

She quickly turned from me.

I looked up at the dazzling billboard advertising sex above her head. Blitz Dance Hall. Immediately I knew I had to lure her away. "We have work." It floated from my mouth as though placed there. Before I knew it, she was walking my way. I smiled again, pleased, and closed the swinging doors behind her.

"God be with you," I said with a nod. She lowered her head and swiftly walked past, leaving an enchanting scent behind. "Next stop, paradise," I announced, and the other workers laughed; some grumbled. They knew a hard day's work was ahead. They were my relief crew. I had picked up a load of men before the sun came up. We were harvesting grain as well as running the orchard and community garden.

I wasn't sure what the mysterious young lady would do at the time, but I knew I couldn't keep my eyes off her. There was a heart-wrenching sadness in her dove-like eyes that made me want to help. Every chance I got, I peeked her way through the rearview mirror. She kept her head low and her hands folded tightly in her lap. She only looked up when we reached the outskirts of town, taking full advantage of the window view as the inner city turned to golden fields.

"HEY BEAUTIFUL, WHAT'S YOUR NAME?" Ma asked, shaking the young lady's hand and giving me a quick, curious glance.

Whenever we brought in workers, Ma came out from the restaurant and welcomed them personally, handing out cups of coffee and some sort of pastry or bread. She knew most of them by name and was vested in their lives. Every now and then, we brought in a woman ready to get her hands dirty doing manual labor. This mysterious woman wearing a crisp white sundress, silver rhinestone trimmed sandals and dangling bangles around her wrist was not ready.

"I'm Ruth," she shyly answered, shielding her face with long wavy, raven black hair.

Being nosy, I lingered around the bus, fidgeting under the hood. *Who is she?* My previous thoughts and worries seemed to float on in her presence.

"Well, Miss Ruth, why don't you follow Tee here into the house," Ma suggested, handing Ruth off to Tante Tita. "She'll get you some clothes and work boots—I think we're about the same size." They were both petite women. Ma smiled kindly. "Don't worry," she patted Ruth's hand, probably sensing her sadness too, "you'll be just fine." Ruth nodded and went with Tante Tita without a fuss as I resurfaced from under the hood.

"Whaas this?" Ma sang, playfully nudging me as I passed by. I guess the silly smile I wore gave my interest in Ruth away.

"Ain't nuttin," I lied, kissing Ma's cheek before walking away. There was a lot to be done.

. . .

Rᴜᴛʜ ᴡᴏʀᴋᴇᴅ ʜᴀʀᴅ. Ma placed her in the orchard, where she spent the day picking fruit and then packing, weighing, and labeling them.

When I found the time, I questioned Mr. Ralph, who collected all the laborers' information. "Who is dat young woman over der?" Ruth was then leaving the fields. "Is she married?"

Mr. Ralph stopped his busy work and replied with a half grin. "She's a widow from Nueva York. I heard from Tita dat her husband died in some sort of incident." He went back to work but made sure to give me all the details I needed. "She left her home-town to see after her mother-in-law...they're staying over in de Ninth Ward." He grunted, lifting a heavy bale of hay onto a conveyor belt, then wiped his forehead. "She asked me dis morning if she could gather behind de combines once she was done in de orchard. She's been hard at work since except for a few minutes rest in the shelter."

"Why the field?" I asked with a puzzled expression. I couldn't imagine why a young lady would want to work in the fields on purpose. Mr. Ralph shrugged his shoulders. The workers were good men. There had never been any harassment incidents, but they were men, and she was a beautiful woman. Besides that, we used big machinery. It wasn't the place for a lady. "Tell de guys to keep an eye out on her, please...and make sure she has everything she needs."

I went over to talk to Ruth.

CHAPTER
TWENTY-SIX

RUTH

Already tired from the day's labor, I sat on the colorful picnic blanket given to me and looked out at the other workers spreading their blankets—laughing and chatting, preparing to eat. It didn't feel like a work environment. Lots of extra attention went into small details that can brighten one's day.

My employer's mother, Ms. Pie, immediately made me feel at home. She gave me comfortable clothes to wear, so I didn't feel out of place amongst the other workers, which left a big first impression on me. Not only was Ms. Pie kind, but I discovered she was a restaurateur who also created and owned a successful beauty line. Needless to say, I was in awe of her. When I worked at Buggy's mom's beauty spa in Harlem, she used Ms. Pie's products. I felt like I was amongst skincare royalty and wanted to consume all I could from her. So, if working on an orchard was my humble beginning back into business ownership, I ran with it.

My day had already been long, but it felt good to work and sweat for a change. Using the buffer zone of silence to think, I dug into the lunch bag they provided, pulled out a juicy red apple, bit into it, and laid back, gazing up at the sky. From where I was situated, up on a hill far away from everyone else, it was the most open blue sky I had ever seen—with the fluffiest white clouds swimming throughout. The trees shading me from the hot Louisiana sun gently swayed against the backdrop. I bit my apple again, thinking, *I've never noticed a tree in sway before.* I know that's hard to believe, but I wasn't the type to notice a tree. I was too busy. Each leaf danced with flickering shadows playing between them, caressing me with its gentle breeze. Before I knew it, my eyes were full of tears. Of all people, the moment made me think of Abuela.

When I was a little girl, Abuela babysat me before I started school. We used to watch telenovelas while she weaved baskets to sell for extra money. It was the only thing she ever successfully and intentionally taught me. They were beautiful intricate hand-crafted designs. I can still smell the weaving straw she used. Walking onto the farm that day took me back. I used to wonder about the place that Abuela never talked about. The place that taught her how to create such beauty—her home in Puerto Rico. And unexpectedly, I stumbled upon the farm I had imagined all those years ago. Its beauty made me cry. It was like a foretaste of heaven—peppered in an assortment of grains, fruits, and vegetables. For me, it was perfect...and I had seen many perfect things.

How many times have I seen the ocean? Laid on white or pink sand? Plenty! I grew angry with myself for taking life's simple pleasures...and people for granted. I never stopped moving long enough to absorb anything. Capturing the perfect picture meant more than being in the moment. The thought of all that wasted energy and how disrespectful Peewee and I were to his mother and her house made me cringe. We spent years high on weed and alcohol, thinking we were living 'the life,' but we were passing the time. More than grieving over Peewee, I was mad. Mad at myself. I should have known better. Peewee was Peewee. He had only just begun to truly live when the time came for him to pay for his mistakes.

But why was I spared, Lord?

Preoccupied with my thoughts, I didn't notice my boss when he sat on the blanket beside me.

"De heavens declare de glory of de Lord, and de sky above proclaims His handiwork." He had Peewee's same accent yet a different tone. I quickly wiped away my tears. "It's okay," he continued, handing me his personal handkerchief from his back pocket. "It brings me to tears too. God's awesome wonders." He gestured toward the beautiful open sky. "My Pa used to call dem pointers...because dey remind us of God's abiding presence." He removed and tilted the cowboy hat on his head in salutation, exposing a head full of slick black curls that seemed to expand upon release. He then laid back on my blanket, biting into an apple. "I'm sorry, can ah join you?" He asked, quickly sitting up and leaning on an elbow, facing me.

"Of course." I leaned in admiration, facing him and thinking of what he said about God creating beautiful things to point to Himself. My eyes dotted across his face. *You are definitely one, my brother.* I handed him back his handkerchief. "Thanks."

"It's all yours—a gentleman always keeps one fuh a lady."

I blushed at his calling me a lady. Ma Nay had spoken that over me. *You're a lady.*

"How's your first day going?" He asked as though there would be more days. That made me smile too.

"I love it here." I instantly shifted my focus, ashamed because I was staring. His eyes were bluer than the ocean, and I couldn't help but dive into them. "Thank you for the opportunity." I fidgeted through my bag, removing a warm sandwich wrapped in butcher's paper, then glanced back at Mr. Bo. He was still reclined on the blanket, wearing simple farming attire that showed a line-backer's build. He smiled, taking another big bite from the apple. His boyish charm released tiny rays of endorphins within me that targeted the dead places. My heart flipped. I took the handker-chief to my forehead.

What the heck is going on here? I wasn't ready to fall for another guy.

"We haven't properly met. I'm Boaz, or Bo." He extended a strong hand that felt glazed over with the evidence of his labor. It took me by surprise. I was used to Peewee's smooth manicured ones.

"Nice to officially meet you, Mr. Bo," I answered, not wanting to go there with his first name yet. "I'm Ruthie Wig— Vega." Wiggins felt distant and unexpectedly odd. I hadn't used it long enough.

"Well, Ms. Ruthie Vega...the pleasure is all mine." Mr. Bo shook my hand with a firm gentleness. "Listen," he added, noticing the pile of sheaves beside my blanket. "Ah heard dat you're interested in gathering de stubble."

"Oh, is that okay?" It never dawned on me that it may be a problem.

"Oh, no, no, it's quite alright." He gestured with his hands, leaning back on his elbows again. "Just make sure not to wander off to anyone else's field; stay with us. There's a lot of machinery out der. I'll warn de guys to keep an eye out for you...and not to mistreat you."

"Thanks," I replied, singing in the back of my head, *brown coco skin—and twirling black hair.* "I appreciate it." I knew I was blush-ing, so I bit into the warm pulled pork sandwich that smelled amazing and gave me something other to do than stare at that gorgeous man.

"No problem," Mr. Bo answered, looking as though he was waiting to see my reaction after tasting the sandwich. He twisted his lips and nodded his head as my eyes widened from the burst of favor. "It's smackin', right?"

"Mmm," I moaned, fumbling for a napkin. The awesome sauce had dripped down my chin. Mr. Bo immediately sat up and wiped it away with his thumb. I blushed again. He smiled, and our eyes briefly locked. He cleared his throat, changing the topic.

"So, what do ya need de straw fuh?"

I swallowed. "Oh, I'm making baskets." I picked up a practice chain that I had started. "Maybe your moms can sell them at the restaurant. I was thinking about weaving some colorful vegetables onto the outside with Gettin' Fresh Cafe weaved above that...you know, for tourists."

"Oh, wow! Ma's gon' love dat."

He laid back on the blanket, tucking his arm behind his head, then took a massive bite of his sandwich. "You know...," he continued, covering his mouth. "You don't have to glean de field for sheaves. We got plenty of it on de old threshing floor. We usually bale the straw for winter bedding." With that, he took another huge bite. "You can use all ya lak," he mumbled.

"Really? That would be great!" I don't know why I was so excited about weaving baskets, but that was the first time I felt encouraged about being in New Orleans. "What have I done to deserve your kindness?" I heard myself asking before thinking. In my head, men always had an agenda. "I mean, I'm a stranger here after all."

"Yes, ah know," Mr. Bo replied, relaxed in the shade. "But ah also know 'bout everything you've done fuh ya mother-in-law since ya husband's death." He said that wide-eyed and sort of shyly. I lowered my head and started weaving anxiously.

The grapevine spreads quickly here.

"Please don't be offended because ah think you're a courageous and kind young lady to leave everything you know to live among complete strangers for someone else's sake." He took a sip of water. I couldn't lift my head from blushing. He continued, "Ah mean, look how you took de initiative to provide fuh ya self and mother-in-law. You didn't consider ya self too proud or embarrassed to work in de fields." He reached out and touched my busy hand. "Ms. Ruthie, ma'am...ah commend you. And may de Lord God Almighty, under whose wings you have come to take refuge, reward you fully fuh what you have done."

My eyes were moist, so I continued to stare into my lap. "Thank you for comforting me with those kind and timely words." He nodded, and feeling at ease around me, placed his cowboy hat over his face.

"You mind if ah catch me some z's while you do ya weaving?"

He was snoring before I could answer.

THAT EVENING I helped Ms. Pie with a computer program they were trying to install. I happened to mention some ideas I felt would benefit their website. Impressed, she asked if I could start helping in the office. They had just lost an employee to maternity leave.

"It's part-time, but you can continue to work in the orchards...or the community garden to help make up hours. As a matter of fact, you should move around the farm, that way you can get a better feel of what we do here.

Just like that, I had a job.

Mr. Bo and Ms. Pie loaded me down with leftovers from the restaurant, then Mr. Bo drove me home on the back of his black 'mirror coated' Kawasaki Ninja H2. I would have never guessed him for a bike guy as country as he was. Him riding a horse would not have fazed me, but a sleek bike that was as sexy as he was made me loopy.

"WHAT THE HECK is going on? Why you so late...and who was that man you were all wrapped up on?" Ma Nay barked as soon as I walked through the door. I had purposely left my cell home. That day, I had a big decision to make and didn't want her input. God gave me His. He put me under His protection at the farm, just as Mr. Bo had stated.

"I found a job," I answered, shutting the blinds. Ms. Gladys was at the window, shamelessly staring out at Mr. Bo through them. He waited until I was in the house safely before driving away.

"Hmph," Ms. Gladys scoffed with a stink face, edging her way toward her wheelchair. She could get around when she wanted to.

"What type of job?" Ma Nay continued, now rummaging through the backpack that I sat down. She picked up a few sheaves. "What's this?"

"I'm working on a farm," I responded, removing my stuff from her hand. I had intended on weaving at night once they dried out.

"A farm?" Ms. Gladys huffed again, turning up her nose. "Ain't no farms around here, girl."

"I know," I responded, giving her back the same attitude and taking half of a homemade pie out of the packed bag. That stopped her questioning instantly. Ms. Gladys inched over in her wheelchair using her dried heels. "The farm's not around here." I continued more respectfully. "I got on a shuttle bus that went out to the country this morning."

133

Ma Nay was so astonished that she stopped picking through the bag.

"Is that safe?" She sat down at the table and eyed over the stuff Ms. Gladys was removing.

"I feel safe. They're cool people."

"Ooh dis here is Ms. Pie's stuff!" Ms. Gladys interrupted. "Destiny used to bring her bourbon pecan chocolate pies home from de weekend market. Ooh, chile! Lawd-have-mercy, dat dere pie was sayin' something—you hear."

"They pay well?" Ma Nay asked, worried about me, not the pies. "You ain't laboring too hard, are you?"

"I promise you, Ma, I feel better than I have in months...and it ain't because of no man," I added, knowing she was still wondering about the guy on the motorcycle. "The farm is just what I needed." Ma Nay smiled wide. "That guy was my boss. I stayed behind to help with a computer program—now I'll be working in the office too."

"Well, go head wit-ya-bad-self!" Ma Nay playfully pushed my arm. I knew she was as concerned as I was about utilizing my degree. "Look at you! I could just hug ya to death." She opened her arms, and we embraced before she moved on to opening the remaining containers of food. Ms. Gladys already had her fork in the greens and potato salad. "Ooh, this is good!" Ma Nay mumbled with a mouth full of field peas. "Real fresh!"

"That's the name of the market, ain't it—Gettin' Fresh?" Ms. Gladys remembered, slapping her hands together. "Real nice people too."

"May the Lord bless the one who helped you!" Ma Nay said, marveling over all the food I brought home.

"His name is Mr. Bo," I revealed, telling my mother-in-law about the man in whose field I had worked. "And yeah, he and his mother were real nice. It was indeed a blessing...because I was going a whole other direction this morning," I said, not intending to tell what I thought of doing first. "Don't even ask," I added before they could fix their mouths to inquire.

"Well, God bless him." Ma Nay cut into the deep dish caramel apple pie. "He's showing his kindness to all of us...including Peewee."

"Yup!" I nodded. "I'll be there until the harvest is completed. God willing, by then, I'll be working full-time in the office until I can figure out where I wanna be in life."

"Good, my daughter. I believe in you. You can do anything when you put your mind to it." Ma Nay patted my arm again, then went back to filling a plate that Ms. Gladys had handed her. "While you're there, stay safe and listen to what you're told. Working outdoors—on a farm at that, ain't easy. It's not ya speed. A lot could go wrong." She looked worried again.

"Don't worry." I assured her, tasting the pie Ms. Gladys was working on. It was good and would require my full attention in bed with some ice cream later. I made sure to cut and save a piece. "Mr. Bo has the workers looking out for me."

"Okay...so it's obvious you've found favor with this Mr. Bo," Ma Nay gathered, examining me with inquisitive eyes. She added, "Do as he says, Ruth," as though coming to a final conclusion. "You might be harassed anywhere else, but you'll be safe there with him."

So I worked in the office and alongside the other workers on Mr. Bo's farm until the end of the barley harvest. Then, I continued working with them through the wheat harvest. And all the while, I lived with my mother-in-law.

CHAPTER
TWENTY-SEVEN

RAHAB

I watched for the next few months as my son came out of his shell and away from his father's shadow. There was an obvious attraction between him and Ruth that couldn't be denied—although they put on as though there wasn't. Shadow watched her closely while he worked, and I saw how Ruth looked at him through sad, longing eyes. Their chemistry was so strong that when we all were together it made me feel like a third wheel.

Shadow and Ruth were always in deep conversation. Every afternoon they took to the shade of an oak tree. And he drove her home every night and kept her bags full of food.

I saw a lot of myself in Ruth; we had the same stories of hurt, despair, and loss. I understood her more than I allowed myself to relate. Ruth's pain brought on memories. It was the way she moved timidly through her day, afraid she'll break. I remembered that fragile state. She moved slowly with Shadow too, which worked in both of their favor. They became good friends allowing time to completely heal and free themselves of their ghosts.

Losing Sal was a nightmare for me. What stopped me from losing my mind was making sure that our son didn't lose his. I worked aimlessly to build our brand so Shadow wouldn't know failure. He couldn't go through any more heartache—yet I couldn't control that; I couldn't secure his heart in bubble wrap. Farming is a difficult line of business, especially for a Black organic farmer. It's a labor of love involving the ever-changing mind of mother nature. You're bound for heartache.

We worked years after Katrina before the land sprung forth bumper crops. Shadow took it all in stride. He continued to plant according to the celestial seasons and insisted the earth knew what it needed. He simply listened. He trained his eyes to know what 'ready' looked like, his nose to smell, his tongue to taste the perfect soil, and he followed the sage advice of his spirit. I could go on and on about Shadow. My mouth lashes out with pride over him. Yes, he understands nature's balance. He understood it better than human conditions. Yet both are unpredictable. To Shadow, the ability to pinpoint an issue and solve it was more appealing. He could interpret the weather signs in the sky, yet he didn't know how to interpret the signs of love. So he stored his own heart in bubble wrap.

When Sal and I bought the farm from Shadow's ex-employer, who fancied him as a son, we planned to take what was already intact and build a family empire. Ten years later, Shadow and I were alone with no legacy in sight. My boy was a great farmer, bright too, but he had no plans of settling down. He was good at the bureaucracy and red tape of running a business. However, he couldn't get out of his own way regarding relationships. He was content with being just like his ex-employer—worked to death with no offspring to leave it all to.

To be fair, I think Shadow and I both used work to jog Sal out of our memories. Still, whereas family, the church, and the guy I started dating kept me grounded—reminding me to breathe, Shadow hid on the farm. I had to stay on top of him. He reverted into a shell until Ruth came along. Then, as his father would say, "He went after her like a duck on a junebug." Shadow quietly wooed Ruth's sadness away.

Unshakeable faith is built on the premise that God's ultimate purpose will come to pass. I knew He had His hand in bringing Ruth and Boaz together.

CHAPTER

TWENTY-EIGHT

RUTH

*Y*o! *Turn your eyes from me...they overwhelm me,* I thought whenever Mr. Bo looked my way. I felt my presence sullied his image. He was too perfect...unlike me, and unlike Peewee. His eyes never flashed with anger. He didn't have an appetite for violence or dishonesty and never spoke a harsh word. Mr. Bo was unlike any man I had ever met. He was different and somehow made me different too. I found myself totally enthralled with him even though he didn't care about trips around the world or name-brand clothes and sneakers. He brightened my mornings with a smile. I felt safe in his presence and okay to be me—the me that was ever-changing and willing to learn. He never made me feel like the misfit I thought of myself. He made me believe in myself again.

I was working full-time at the office and enjoying every minute. The former staff member and her new family had moved out of state. Who would have thought that working on a farm

139

would be my forte? I loved it! From doing the accounting, working on the website presence, creating social media content, to helping out with the orchard and garden. It all was magic. I helped in bringing that forth and got to use my skills while making new friends in a dream location.

My favorite part of the day was the bike ride home with Mr. Bo. I closed my eyes, wrapped my arms around his waist, and pressed my cheek into his back. He smelled like outdoors—hard work and determination. We didn't talk, even though our helmets were equipped with Bluetooth communication. A conversation wasn't needed. I heard and saw everything I needed to know about him—from the music he listened to, the lyrics he openly chose to sing, and the twisting golden field roads he drove for miles and miles and miles. All of it was his language. And I must admit, I liked it all. I was coming alive again.

"You know you can call me Bo if you lak, right?" We were on a blanket, under our oak tree, taking a break from a long day's work. Mr. Bo was leaning back against the tree, eating an apple. "Ah consider us friends." He added because I hesitated to respond.

"Yes, we are," I said with enthusiasm, yet I knew that I owed him an explanation as to why I was holding back on our friend-ship. I laid down my work and looked him directly in his enchanting blue eyes. I wanted to say, *I long to be touched by you—you fine specimen of a man. Ay, papi, take me; my dreams are consumed by you.* My more rational thoughts said—*too soon*, even though my entire body stood in agreement against it. Instead, I said, "I don't know why, but ever since my husband died, I've been feeling guilty about moving on and making friends." I lowered my eyes. It felt silly saying it out loud like Peewee was physically there, holding me back from proceeding with life. "I know it's stupid." I started weaving again.

"Ah don't think it's stupid." Mr. Bo sat up from the tree, stern-faced. "Ah felt de same way when my pa died...and ah wasted ten years living in misery and loneliness." I looked up at him. The tone in his voice had changed. It sounded sad and sincere. "Please don't think dat I'm telling you what to do...but ah wouldn't wish dat type of torment on my worst enemy," he continued as I nervously weaved faster. I had strong feelings for him that I was suppressing. "And ah know dat my pa wouldn't be pleased with me acting lak dat either...but ah just couldn't move fo'ward..." he stopped my hands from weaving. At that time, I had already completed ten baskets. Ms. Pie sold them all as I predicted. She bundled them with fresh fruits and vegetables, some with home-made goods. They sold quickly. "I couldn't move forward until I met you, Ruth." I peeked Mr. Bo's way. His eyes were fixed on me in a way that spoke volumes. He touched my face, and I sighed heavily. "Ms. Ruth..."

My heart raced. *We're friends,* I told myself. *I live for his conversation and company.*

"Pretty lady, before ah met you..." He paused, looking away and breaking the magnetic pull my lips felt. "...before ah met you, ah wasn't messin' wit nobody...ah was...Ruthless!" He said as though it was a second thought. He chuckled. "Get it? Ruth-less?" He burst into laughter over himself.

"I hate you," I responded, half laughing. He played too much. I was red with embarrassment and ashamed of myself for thinking otherwise. At the same time, I was relieved. I wasn't mentally ready for a relationship, but I missed the feeling of being in a man's arms. The warmth of a caress. *Besides*, I thought, making my feelings logical, *any woman with half a mind would want to be with Bo.*

When I think about it, I should have known his true feelings toward me. They were in the way he fawned over me. And if I couldn't sense that, I should have known by the backpack on my back full of food every night showing me he cared. We were hiccups in each other's day-to-day existence, as well as the water we both needed.

CHAPTER

TWENTY-NINE

BOAZ

I loved everything about Ruth, and that was uncommon for me. She was rare, different from any other woman I had ever dealt with. Her right arm was sleeved in tattoos. Her ears were lined with piercings. Nothing about her said traditional or safe. Everything had an edge of flair. Yet she was as dainty and frail as a newborn fawn. She squealed at the sight of dragonflies, and smelled like melons and honeydew.

There was something about Ruth. Something that haunted me in my sleep and lured me through the day. Something that pulled back my tough disapproving exterior and warmed my heart. The thought of her often ran through my mind. Because of her, I knew love again. And love was making a fool of me. I came across as weird, silly, and awkward—yet dark places were lit within me in her presence. You look at life differently when love is standing by your side. I believe I was asleep until Ruth.

I drove her home every night on the back of my bike. When

143

she wrapped her arms around my waist, I decided instantly that I was taking her the long way just to be in her company. Being with Ruth felt like a mini trip to heaven. I know it sounds corny, but I felt lighter around her. Free to be me. No one was putting on airs. There were no worries, just she and I. From day one, I knew I wanted to take care of her.

At mealtime, I called to her, "Ruth come over here and help yourself to some food!"

THIRTY

RUTH

He sat me down at his family's booth nearest the storefront window. His mother served me plate after plate of the most delicious and fresh food I'd ever tasted. Ma Nay was a good cook, but Ms. Pie slayed with the farm-fresh ingredients.

"How you lak de brisket?" Bo asked after making his usual table rounds. Everyone in the restaurant knew him and vied for his attention.

"So tender," I answered. The smoked meat was like butter.

"Tender like a woman's heart." He winked, tipping and then removing his hat as he took a seat across from me. I gave him 'the eye,' and we snickered. He was as corny as the buttered corn on my plate.

As soon as Bo sat down, Ms. Pie had his favorite meal delivered to the table. The 'Rock Da Bell Peppers' stuffed with a surf and turf jambalaya mixture and covered in melted gouda. A side of rustic potato salad, and sweet potato hush puppies glazed with homemade cinnamon honey butter.

The way Ms. Pie cooked and maneuvered around the place made me think of how excited Peewee was dreaming of his mom coming to cook at our club.

"This place is great," I said, feeling nostalgic. Gettin' Fresh Cafe had that magic element; I could feel it. All the locals and tourists traveling past the city limits for a taste of a melting pot of culture wrapped in Creole goodness could feel it too. The dishes didn't simply have catchy hook names. They were plated with the excellence of a Michelin Star restaurant. When you visited, not only did you get fresh garden food, you got an experience—from the scenery to the mix-tapes playing in the background. It was unique. Truly a 'destination find' restaurant.

"Coot! Dat ting rite dere is good!" Mr. Bo said, digging in immediately. "Every bite is lak de first time." He shook his head, piling his fork with some of everything.

"Easy, cowboy." Ms. Pie insisted, coming over and pouring two tall glasses of 'Just Like Dat' pineapple sweet tea. Bo wrapped his arm around her waist sideways. She was an attractive and hip woman, hardly old enough to be the mother of such a burly man. She wore her golden locs in a curly asymmetrical pixie cut. Her aprons were customized by a local artist, displaying inner-city women's faces and styles. Ms. Pie had swag.

"You put ya foot in it dis time, Ma!" Bo said with his mouth full.

Ms. Pie bent, kissing his forehead. "He says that every time," she replied, tussling his locs before whipping out a kitchen towel from her apron to hit him. "Slow down, boy! You eat worse than ya pa did."

I watched them and thought of what Ma Nay would say about

how the way to a man's heart is through his stomach. There was definitely something to that.

"How did you learn to cook like this?" I asked. The 'Flyy Chick 'n' Waffles' doused with spicy 'Uptown Syrup Butta' was slammin!

Ms. Pie scooted Bo over and took a seat. "Welp, growing up—
—"

"Oh lawd, here she goes." Bo shook his head and popped a piece of strayed cornbread in his mouth.

"Hush," she laughed. "Like I was saying," she playfully rolled her eyes at Bo. "Growing up, it was just my Big Mama and me...she's the one I named the cosmetic company after. Lotti. Anyhow, I was always underfoot, and Big Mama was always cooking and creating recipes with fresh herbs and garden vegetables. She was big into holistic living way before 'organic' was a thing. When Big Mama died, I was relocated to the Bronx and helped in raising my siblings. My moms can't cook to save her life," she laughed. "Thank Goodness, I loved the kitchen." Ms. Pie slowed down telling the story she had probably told a million times. She pulled a napkin from the dispenser on the table, taking it to her wet eyes. Bo threw an arm around her shoulder, continuing to drink his tea.

"Back then, my life was out of control," Ms. Pie continued, remembering something hurtful. My eyes grew moist right away because I felt the connection. "Food and dance were the only things I could control," she looked into my eyes, handing me a napkin too. "Sort of like them baskets you've been weaving. My food makes people happy...and it makes me happy feeding them." Ms. Pie patted my hand; someone was calling her to the back of the restaurant. "This too shall pass," she concluded, standing. She was needed on the phone. Ms. Pie gave Bo a wink, passing the baton to him.

Bo cleared his throat. "Told you she reminds me of you." He handed me another napkin. "Y'all both crybabies." He made me laugh, and I snorted, which made me laugh harder. I didn't want to feel sad because I was having a good time.

"What's there to do around here?" I asked, dabbing my eyes. I hadn't been out in months.

"Ain't nothing happenin' round here..." he answered, spooning up some banana foster cream pie. "This town is so small you can spit across it—dey pull de sidewalks in by six." He sort of chuckled. I dropped my eyes. Deep inside, I think I wanted him to ask me out.

"Every now and den, someone might throw a fais doo doo—lak a party." He went on, but my mind was elsewhere.

Do I want him to ask me out?

"We 'bout to have de end of harvest festival...and you already know dat," he added, remembering I worked in the office and ordered the supplies. "Dat's a big deal round here. De day after, we givin' Paw-Paw a birthday party. You ain't met him yet, have you?" He didn't give me a chance to answer "Ah now you'll lak him. God willing, he'll be turning eighty-five. De whole family is comin' down and ev'rything." He lowered his eyes. "You can come through if you want?" It seemed harmless. "I'd lak if you did. I'd lak to meet ya mama-n-em."

I smiled. The idea of Ma Nay getting out and enjoying festivities sweetened the pot and delighted me.

"We'd love to."

CHAPTER
THIRTY-ONE

RUTH

The night of the festival, Ma Nay came into the bedroom we shared and said to me, "Ruth, my daughter, it's time that you let go of that thing inside that judges you from the outside." We were supposed to be getting ready. We missed the morning activities because we had to rush Ms. Gladys to the emergency room. She fell down the front steps and broke her arm. She had been falling a lot.

"What are you talking about, lady?" I responded to Ma Nay. I was trying to unhook my bracelet so I could take a shower.

"It's only you getting in your own way, you know?" She sat on the edge of the bed and motioned for me to hand her my arm. "I know you loved Peewee." Her tone lowered. It was still hard for her to talk about the boys.

"Ma Nay—"

"No, I want you to listen." She unlatched the bracelet and then slightly tugged my arm. "Sit down, Ruthie." I took a seat. Immediately the tears fell. I knew she was giving me her blessings to move forward. "The love you guys had ain't never going nowhere. You'll always have that place in your heart for Peewee..." She patted my hand as she looked at me straight on. "I see that sparkle in your eyes for Mr. Bo...and well, he's here in the flesh today." Ma Nay drew me in her arms, which made me cry outwardly. "There, there." She patted my back. "Life is short, honey. You and I know that more than most. Don't waste what time you have crying over the past."

I was trying to compose myself. "Ma, I know...but I can't help how I feel, and—"

"And feelings can be a hell-of-a thing—I know! They can be the spirit of joy lifting you up one minute, or the spirit of discontent ruining your life the next. Been there. Done that. Ruth, Mr. Bo has been extremely kind. He's gone above and beyond for you. Obviously, he likes you...and I'll be bold enough and say that I think he loves you...you do too, don't you?" I didn't respond. I felt embarrassed thinking of another man so soon after Peewee. Ma Nay pulled from our embrace and looked me dead in the eyes. "I'm okay with you moving on, Ruth. Really, I am. My only desire is your happiness." She smiled with a sincerity that touched my heart. I loved that woman and longed to make her happy.

"You're right, Ma," I said, standing and wiping my tears. "I do like Mr. Bo...Bo. We've become really good friends, and I don't wanna mess that up," I added, turning on my heels toward the dresser to place my bracelet down. I caught a glimpse of myself in the mirror and ran my fingers through my lifeless hair. It hadn't had any TLC since leaving New York. I let everything go. I was older than I was yesterday and definitely aged since Peewee. Time was flying, and I knew my biological clock was ticking. I wasn't a teenager anymore; thirty was knocking on the door. I wanted to be a mother and wife with someone like Boaz.

But, can Bo want to be with a girl like me? I know I'm worthy of love, but am I worthy of his? Are my doubts foolish?

Ma Nay shook her head, stood, and looked at me through the mirror. "I can see the wheels turning in your head. That thing speaking to you from the inside again. Ruth, you are worthy of Mr. Bo. If God knows every thought, every mistake, every mishap, yet He calls you a masterpiece, what makes Mr. Bo any better?" She motioned with expressive hands. "Now, do as I tell you," she said, touching my back and ignoring my fears. "Take a nice bath, put on some sweet smelling perfume, and dress in your nicest clothes. Get real cute. Then, go to that festival and GET...YA...MAN! Tell me all about it when you get back." She slid in, closing her mouth with a smile that read 'accomplished'.

"Wait, you're not going?" I spun toward her.

"No, I can't—Gladys needs me here...and to be honest, I can't do all that standing either." I looked disappointed. "Don't worry, God willing, I'll be there tomorrow for the birthday party."

"Then I'm not going!" I plopped down on the bed we shared, pouting. Ma Nay was my excuse for going and my safety net.

"The hell you say!" Ma Nay yanked me upright. "You going!" She motioned for me to stand. "Come on, get up. You'll thank me one day." I stood grudgingly. "You can always find an excuse if you look for one. Stop doing that!" She held my face, making me look directly into her bulging brown eyes. "The worst that can happen is you'll have a great time...and trust me, Ruth; I want you to have a GREAT time." She turned me toward the mirror again. "You are worthy, and you deserve this." I tilted my head and smiled at the woman in the mirror. Ma Nay was right. "All you have to do is stand back and notice what Mr. Bo is doing. Don't be all up on him," she added, tapping my nose, "when you can find some time alone, take it! He'll make the next move—if he likes you like I know he does."

I sighed deeply. "All right!" *YOLO.* I threw my hands up in surrender. "I'll do everything you say." Ma Nay was indeed a mother to me.

So I went down to the festival that night and followed the instructions of my mother-in-law. I ate and drank amongst new friends and had a good time.

AFTER BO FINISHED EATING and drinking and was in good spirits, himself, he laid against our tree, waiting. I took a deep breath and walked up the hill toward him, sensing he was waiting for me. I quietly tip-toed up on him, then removed the hat covering his face.

"Howdy, cowboy," I said, feathering his hair before placing his hat back. He chuckled.

"Who dat stranger?" He jokingly asked, playfully grabbing me around the legs, making me fall against him. We awkwardly laughed and I pushed myself from his chest, sensing I had been greatly missed. I had purposely stayed away, just as Ma Nay suggested, watching him from afar as he entertained and talked with guests.

I leaned against Bo, allowing him to throw his arm across my shoulders and pull me near. It was almost time for the fireworks. The air was thick with the smell of barbecue and funnel cakes. The usual night sounds were drowned out by the crowd's merriment and the hired DJ. Bo and I gazed out at the sky, lit up by the lights of the carnival rides.

"I'm sorry I missed everything earlier." I had texted him about Ms. Gladys. He texted back, concerned, saying that he could build her a ramp to quickly get in and out of the house.

"How is she?" He rested his chin on top of my head. I nervously fidgeted with my hair, hoping it didn't smell like the cigarettes the group I was hanging out with was smoking. "She broke her arm," I answered.

"Oh, no!" He pulled himself from the comfy position we shared, concerned for Ms. Gladys. "Sorry to hear that. Is she okay?"

"Pfft! Yeah, she's a tough old coot," Ms. Gladys and I were frenemies. We loved getting on each other's nerves, which was how Ma Nay and I started out. "She's home resting with my mother-in-law."

"Well, dat's good. I'll get dat ramp built for her on Monday...you know, because of Paw-Paw's party tomorrow. You still coming, right?"

"Of course. My mother-in-law too."

He smiled brightly, resting his chin back against my head. "Dat's good."

"I heard you got dunked by ya moms in the dunking tank today," I said, laughing, imagining the sight. "Sorry I missed that."

He chuckled. "Oh, you think dat's funny, huh?" He began tickling me.

"Okay, okay!" I pleaded, worming from his grasp. Suddenly, I heard what the DJ was playing. "Ooh, wait, that's my song!" I yelled, standing and reaching for Bo's hands.

The last song of the evening was playing. "Very Special" by Debra Lawson. Coincidently, it was the same song that ended the radio program each night that my mother used to listen to. I took it as a sign and extended my hands to Bo. *Leap, and he will follow,* as Ma Nay said.

Instantly Bo spaced out into his awkwardness. His mouth fell open.

"What? You can't dance?" I asked, egging him on.

He grinned, handsomely. "Can ah dance?" He smugly replied,

taking my hands to stand. "I'll have you know dat no one is admitted in my family without a 'can dance' card.

"Mhmm," I mouthed as he spun me lightly before drawing me tautly against his body.

At first touch, he quivered and I flinched, drawing my fingers back. We awkwardly laughed. Trying again, Bo looked down at me with admiration in his eyes and pulled me close, cupping my hand into his. I exhaled, resting my head against his pounding chest. Our breaths came quicker and shorter. Bo made an outward sigh before we both relaxed in the embrace. "All my life, I have looked for you," Debra sang and the music swelled as we danced under the stars.

The fireworks show started before the song ended, startling us. We awkwardly laughed again, stepping back from each other, embarrassed by the thoughts we visited in our minds.

"That DJ's good," I said, turning from him, feeling blushed like a middle school girl with a crush. "Where did y'all find him?" I asked, clearing my throat and pretending to look down on the festivities—walking away. I didn't recall the DJ's information on file when I did the budgeting.

"Hmph." I could hear Bo shuffling his feet on the ground, kicking up dried leaves as he walked toward me. "Dat's Mama's lil boyfriend." He turned me around by the waist and then removed his hat. "I'm not s'posed to know 'bout-em." He pulled me close. We began swaying, smiling at each other, and falling in love. "Some DJ from New York...an old friend, she says." The heat between Bo and I was electric.

With stumbling words I confessed, "I like you."

Bo bit down on his lip. "I like you too."

I shyly smiled. "I mean, I really like you." My shy smile turned coy. Before he could respond, I jumped with the confidence of three beers under me and kissed his supple lips. His eyes widened, and his silence became deafening. We searched each other's eyes for words.

"May de Lord bless you, Ruth." He finally said in a proud voice. "You are showing more family loyalty and moral character now more den ever. You can have any guy you want. Rich or poor. But you chose me—awkward and committed to God, family, and legacy...thank you," he said as though astonished. "You're a virtuous woman. Ah wanna do right by you."

My tears fell. It wasn't about what Bo said but the attitude of his heart. He lowered himself and pulled me into a magical kiss. At that moment, everything changed. I was fully vested. Bo lifted me off my feet and spun me around with joy.

"I'm gonna marry you one day," he hastily said, smiling with the same smile that enchanted me from the beginning.

In a heartbeat, I thought, feeling I trusted and loved him. He had cemented his place in my heart.

We kissed again. This time with pent-up desires. I knew I wanted Bo, and I could feel he wanted me too, yet he showed the incredible restraint I often lacked. Giving intimacies instead of lovemaking. He eased away from my snake-like hands that were pleased with the chance to finally touch him.

"Come on," he put his hat back on and took my hand, tenderly kissing it. "You can't go back to your mother-in-law empty-handed."

We trotted down the hill together hand-in-hand.

PART: THREE

And Naomi had a kinsman of her husband's, a mighty man of wealth,
of the family of Elimelech, and his name was Boaz.
Ruth 2:1

CHAPTER

THIRTY-TWO

RUTH

I had never been to The Big House. Bo used to live there with both his parents. After his father passed, he and his mother built a smaller farm-style home near the fields. They only opened The Big House for family occasions and to visitors.

"Sugar, Honey, Ice, Tea...will you look at this!" Ma Nay excitedly proclaimed, attempting to end her cursing. "This feels unbelievable...like we're at Southfork or the Ponderosa or somewhere." She laughed, slapping her thigh with a hoot. "Shoot, any minute JR's fitna walk out with Little Joe, Hoss, or Sue Ellen 'em.

It was that grand. Although Ma Nay exaggerated, it was nicer than anything we'd ever seen or lived in. The lawn was neatly groomed; where it ended, a thick field of fragrant lavender grew, and a big white Antebellum-style house lined with striking decorative columns sat in the middle of everything. Indeed it was a mansion. At that moment, I realized Bo was not average at all. He and Ms. Pie were rich.

"Hola!" Tita called to me, getting out of her car. She and the family had attended a service at their home church that morning. We were invited; however, Ma Nay only attended Greater Zion Community Church. She said she spent ten years away and planned on never leaving it again.

"Hola! Sorry, we're late," I responded to Tita, shutting the car door. Ms. Gladys had lent us her vehicle. "We got a little turned around." The location was definitely off the grid, intertwined within the farm's vicinity.

"You're good. We're not all here yet, either," Tita answered, hugging my neck as I approached her car. "Que linda, look at you," she said, quickly giving me a 'go gurl' look.

"Thank you, thank you," I smiled, posing and laughing. "Tita, this is my mother-in-law, Naomi Wiggins," I said, standing between them, gesturing with my hands. "Ma, this is Tita—Bo's aunt."

"Hellur," Ma Nay half answered, acting differently, putting on airs—trying to be dignified.

"Hi, Mrs. Wiggins," Tita responded, hugging Ma Nay's neck. "You look familiar."

"You too." She responded, looking over her glasses, eying Tita. "Hmm, maybe not." That was Ma Nay—you had to earn her trust and friendship.

We began the walk to The Big House. The tree-lined driveway went on and on. I couldn't help but dream about living in a house like that with a man like Bo; then he appeared on the front porch and yelled, "Hey!" Waving his hat to get our attention. "Come in this way!" Tita was taking us around back to where the festivities had already begun. I could hear music and people talking. "I got someone here I want you to meet," Bo added.

"Y'all go ahead." Tita had noticed someone she wanted to catch up with. "We'll talk later, Mami."

159

"Okay." I responded, gleefully. I liked Tita. She was originally from New York, too, Alphabet City. She wasn't Bo's real aunt but an older Latina family friend and chain smoker like Ma Nay. They were always trying to quit.

"Oh Lord, I hope I can act right." Ma Nay whispered from the side of her mouth as we continued to walk.

"Oh, stop!" I slapped her busy hands from constantly fixing herself. She was a mess.

"I'm serious! These people are beautiful."

"Yeah, well, now you know why I feel like such an outcast."

She stopped walking and turned to look at me. "No, darling. You belong," she said, trying to catch her breath. It was a good walk for her. "Look at you!" I had put on some makeup and splurged on an outfit. Ma Nay and I were saving for a vehicle. Clothes weren't as essential as they once were to me, but it did feel good slipping into some new swag. Ma Nay threw her arm around my shoulder. "You just as pretty as you wanna be," she added, continuing to walk.

"You aren't slight either," I said, using one of her lines. We laughed.

Bo greeted us with a charming smile. "Good afternoon, ladies." He held the door open. "Please come in." Ma Nay walked through first, rudely staring. He tipped his hat, "Ma'am," he said to her, then smiled wider at me. We gave each other a quick peck on the cheek. "You look good," he whispered.

"You too," I smiled. He did. Bo was cleaner than the board of health, in a pressed button-down shirt, slacks, and his hair neatly cornrowed back into two braids with the sides and edges freshly faded and lined. It was the perfect style for highlighting his amazing eyes and chiseled features.

"Paw-Paw," Bo said louder than necessary, shutting the door.

"We got company!" He touched our backs lightly and walked us into a sitting room off the foyer.

The home was grand and elegantly decorated. It didn't look like Bo or Ms. Pie. The farmhouse where they lived and I worked suited them more. Yet I was wide-eyed in awe over my surroundings. Ma Nay was more fascinated with Bo; she looked at him like she saw a ghost.

"Who dat, Shadow? The older man, neatly suited and sitting in an armchair near a fireplace asked—calling Bo by the nickname Ms. Pie used in private from time to time.

Ma Nay stopped in her tracks and turned, looking at Bo again. Her face read of disbelief.

"Shadow?" She clasped her mouth. "Well, blow me down and call me shorty. Boy, it's you! Don't you look just like your daddy." She grabbed Bo and hugged him tightly. He stood stiff in her arms, clueless.

CHAPTER
THIRTY-THREE

NAOMI

"Who dat? Y'all come closer," Uncle repeated. "My eyes ain't what dey used to be."

"Oh my goodness!" I yelled, walking into the sitting room sleeved in mahogany walls and shelved leather bound books. "I can't believe it!" I couldn't. It felt like a surprise homecoming. I hadn't seen or heard from any of Eli's family since we left New Orleans ten years ago. Uncle and I had kept up for a while, but due to my depression, I cut him off.

"Hi, Unk!" I said excitedly, standing in front of him.

"Lord, chile, is that you, Nay?" He stood with Shadow's help and extended his shaky, feeble arms. He still had an aura of light around him.

"Yes, sir, it's me!" We hugged.

"Well, ain't you a sight for sore eyes."

"Unk, you don't even know."

"Where's the boys?" He turned slightly, eagerly looking for Peewee and Junnie. That jabbed my heart in a way I can't explain.

Already emotional, my eyes instantly swelled with tears. I contorted my face in agony and shook my head—the words wouldn't even form in my mouth. Ruth rubbed my back, reminding me that she was there. Uncle's mind was sharp as a tack. He understood and dropped his head, not wanting me to see his sadness. Eli and the boys were the only connections left to his deceased sister and the end of their bloodline. Uncle and the late First Lady had adopted Sal at birth. They never did have children.

He cleared his throat. "Well, who is dis lovely young lady?" he asked, noticing Ruth with a full denture smile. I quickly wiped away my tears and smiled as well.

"This is my daughter-in-love, Ruth, Peewee's bride." Shadow's eyes grew. He choked and began coughing.

"You, okay," Ruth asked, patting him. He was coughing up a lung but gestured with his hand that he was alright.

"Bless your heart. Well, hello, sweetheart." Uncle issued towards Ruth, ignoring everything else. He took a few weak steps forward to greet her properly.

"Hello," Ruth answered, still worrying over Shadow but indulging Uncle's sentiments.

"And you remained with your mother-in-law, huh?" Uncle continued totally focused on Ruth.

"Yes, sir." She smiled awkwardly. Shadow had his head tilted, staring at her in disbelief. I guessed he figured out who I was. I knew my boys weren't much to write about, but they were mine.

"Well, ain't you a blessing, sweetheart." Uncle held Ruth by the hand and wouldn't let go. "And you know my grandson, Boaz?"

"Yes, sir. He's the reason we're here." I could tell she was crumbling, doubting herself under scrutiny. "I'm working for Bo and his mom at the farm."

"Look at God!" Uncle smiled, letting her hand go and focusing on Shadow with a stern face. "What's wrong wit-chew, boy?"

"Nuttin', Paw-Paw," he answered quickly, coming out of his shock. "What-you-need?"

"Help me sit down, will ya," Uncle whispered, grabbing Shadow's arm for support in getting back to his chair. "Why don't y'all go join de festivities and let me and Nay catch up." He plopped in his seat. "Nay, pull up a chair, darlin'."

Faith doesn't ask you to know—it asks you to believe. God definitely had a plan in everything going on. I motioned for Ruth to lift her chin up as she anxiously walked out of the room, following behind Shadow.

"A bird in de hand is worth more den two in a bush, huh?" Uncle said, referring to Ruth and my situation. He was still wise.

THIRTY-FOUR

RUTH

"So, Cousin Peewee was your husband?" Bo sort of asked, glancing back at me. We quickly walked through the open-floor planned home, passing many beautiful rooms. Bo wasn't being rude, just acting weirder than usual. It made me feel uncomfortable. I would have rathered a tour. "I'm sorry, I'm just...ah guess I'm in shock," he confessed, turning his head to look at me again.

"Yeah, I get it. What a coincidence, huh?" I crossed and rubbed my arms, comforting myself. "But yes, to answer your question, Mahlon and I were married," I replied, giving Peewee's name some dignity. I wasn't ashamed of my husband but I did worry if Bo found him unacceptable. *I wish O was here.* She always knew what to say and do.

"Wow!" Bo made a mind-blown hand motion over his head. "Poof!" We awkwardly laughed together. "I'm sorry, ah just have so many questions." He stopped walking and tenderly rubbed his hand on my shoulder, letting me know he meant no harm.

"Me too, actually." I leaned against the wall. "Like, how are you all related?" They had no family resemblance.

"Ahh, let me see." He scratched his head, thinking. "First cousins...once removed on my dad's side. Peewee and Junnie's dad...was...Paw-Paw's nephew. We only met once." He shook his head. "Ah faintly remember 'em. We met after Katrina—before dey moved to de city. How did dey die, ah mean what happened?" He looked concerned. I lowered my head.

"Well——"

"You know what? Scratch dat. I'm sorry, dat's awkward. Dis isn't de time." He pulled me in. "Ah don't wanna overwhelm you." He gave me the biggest bear hug. It felt like I'm sorry for your loss and I love you simultaneously. I sighed and nervously laughed again; tears were on the brink of falling. I was trying to act normal, but everything felt so unfamiliar.

"You okay," he asked, coming from the hug and lowering himself to look at me directly. "This is okay...we're okay. We are okay, right?" He asked, concerned.

"Of course." I covertly wiped my eyes and exhaled. "That was just...awkward. My mother-in-law is still very sensitive." Bo didn't fully believe me.

"Ruth, I'm your friend first. If you say pump de brakes, we pump 'em. Ah understand de need for time."

"Thank you...," I respected him even further, "but full speed ahead, please." We smiled with fondness and hugged again, taking in each other's scents and ending with a soft kiss on the lips. It reminded me of how much I was into him. My body temperature instantly rose, and I felt flushed. I had never waited to be with a man like that before.

"Mmm," Bo moaned, his eyes briefly dotted mine. He sighed.

"Let me introduce you to de rest of de family...before ah get in trouble. Let's see if you know any more of 'em!" He joked.

We continued walking to the back of the house, now hand-in-hand. Bo opened the patio door off the kitchen and kissed my cheek as I walked out under his outstretched arm. There was a large gated pool surrounded by a yard full of unfamiliar people, but what caught my eye was the array of familiar ones spread throughout the oversized deck. I stood in disbelief.

This can not be happening.

"¡Ay coño! What is this?" I blurted out what was meant as my inner thoughts. It felt like a bad episode of Punked or This Is Your Life.

"Ruth, dis is my family!" Bo proudly announced. "Family dis is my lady friend, Ruth." Someone stopped the music and Luther came to a screeching halt.

"Ruth!" They all yelled.

Lorah ran over first and tightly hugged my neck. She was my ex-boyfriend, Buggy's sister—Lo-boogie is what we used to call her. She had a baby hanging from her leg, one riding her full hips, and one in the oven. There was Jez, her older brother. He had matured into a man and looked just like Mr. Zee, his father who picked me up and spun me around. I was already dizzy. I searched Bo's face, but he looked as clueless as I was.

"Wait, y'all know Ruth?" I heard him ask Chris, Buggy's cousin. They were really close back in the days. I remembered them competing to see who could do the most chin-ups hanging from the stop light before games. Chris even dated O for a sec. She was too much for him, though. He preferred church girls. His father, Pastor Sy, Buggy's uncle, hosted summer block parties for the neighborhood kids on Charlotte Street. Chris's mother, Mrs. Lydia, used to get her hair and treatments done at the spa where I worked. She brought homemade empanadas in for the staff and pasteles and coquito during the holidays. Buggy's mom, Mrs. Go, who at the time was acting standoffish—giving me the stink eye, owned the beauty spa. The spa I worked in that sold and used Ms. Pie's products.

Ms. Pie's products, I thought before Buggy showed up from behind. He quickly dipped me in his arms, forcing a hard, wet, lingering kiss upon me.

"Whoo! Yo, what you doing?" Bo had his hands firmly gripped into Buggy's shoulders, pulling him off.

Buggy stopped and brought me up into his arms. He wore a smug look on his face like he was doing me a favor. He squeezed me tightly. It's funny because I wormed in his grip, yet I wanted to cling to him. He, and the scent of his CK One cologne were the only things there that felt safe at the moment.

"This ya girl, cuz?" he asked, looking slick. His breath smelled like he had started the party a bit early.

"Yeah," Bo answered, puffing his chest.

Buggy fully released me. "Is she really?" He moistened his lips and ran a thumb across my cheek. "Cause she used to be my girl."

This was a woman's nightmare.

Bo dotted my eyes again, this time looking for anything to deny the charges. "Lak you said, used to be," he answered less spiritedly. I could tell he was disappointed. We hadn't had the chance to discuss past relationships.

"Hmph," Buggy uttered unbothered. He crossed his arms over his broad chest; he was well into a drunken state and readying to start something. "Man, we used to have some good times and big dreams, right, Ruthie?" I lowered my head to keep my eyes off of him. Despite everything happening he was still Buggy the super-star—always flossin', rockin' the latest gear, girls jockin'—fine. "I kept my part of the deal..." he added, being relentless. "I can give you anything your heart desires."

"We good," Bo took my hand and made a fist with his other to give Buggy a pound goodbye.

Buggy ignored his gesture. "I'm curious, you good with all this, Ruthie?" Against my better judgment, I looked up into his eyes. Buggy intimately knew the voices in my head telling me to do otherwise. "I mean, I never took you as a...farm girl."

For a split second, I saw everything that glitters and made sense in Buggy, and me indulging in all its ratchetness. In the moment, he shined brighter than the billboard at Blitz Dance Hall. He was the easy way out. Familiar and dangerous. Bo must have noticed the look on my face because he released my hand.

"Bo!" Someone called from the kitchen door. "Your grandfather is asking for you."

"Excuse me," he said in a hushed voice. "I'll be back." Before I could retrieve my character, he was gone.

CHAPTER
THIRTY-FIVE

RAHAB

"So you just gonna drop Ruth like yesterday's news?" I asked Shadow. He had entered the room where I was changing —ranting and raving.

After church, the family had gathered on the property for professional pictures, taking advantage of everyone being together in one place. We had lost and gained so many beloved members since our last group photo that it felt like the perfect timing to update the albums. What better event than celebrating life? Poppa Josh was a blessed eighty-five-year-old.

"Ma, you won't dere," Shadow complained, removing his church shoes to change also. "Ah can't compete with Liam," he tossed a shoe down. "He's a superstar. I'm just...me," he added. 'Me' had always been enough before.

Buggy—the family called him Liam, short for William, was a starter for the Los Angeles Clippers. He had the 'it' factor that made for good television. Talent. Drama. Looks. We were all very proud of him. He had turned himself into a big sports personality. You couldn't tell him anything; he was so full of himself.

As children, he and Shadow were close as brothers. Their grandparents, Tante Maw-Maw and Poppa Will cared for them along with Chris every summer. They spoiled them rotten. The three stooges, we called them. When Liam started playing ball for different leagues, he stopped coming to Baton Rouge for the summer. He came only once or twice a year with the rest of the family for our annual reunions and alternated Thanksgivings. Somewhere along the line he and Shadow became rivals, especially after Sal's death. It was my kid sister, Go-Go, and me all over again. It didn't help that Liam was just like his real father—a piece of work.

"Has Ruth ever asked you to be more than who you are?" I hated to see Shadow beating himself up.

"No...but den dere's dis whole Peewee thing, too." He added, reaching for any reason to guard his heart as he changed into a graphic tee. "Do you remember Peewee, Mama? Maybe Ruth is just out of my league. Actions speak louder den words. She's obviously about dat life. I'm a simple man." He spread his arms, displaying himself before topping his new outfit off with his dad's cowboy hat.

I walked over and threw my arms around Shadow's waist. I knew he was hurting. He went out on a limb and made himself vulnerable to love after pushing it away for so long.

"Son, must I remind you that once upon a time, I was called a prostitute." I hated to remind him, or myself of my scandalous past. However, I remembered how it felt to be judged because of your choices and circumstances. People called you out of your name and made you feel the part.

"Dat's not de same, Ma."

"It's exactly the same, baby. The past always has a way of

catching up, and there's no way we can change it. It is what it is. Ruth had no idea that you all were related. You can't convict her for living life before you. Besides, you and your cousins haven't been close in years." I turned to pick up our clothes scattered around the room. "When was the last time you and Liam checked in?" I gave Shadow the eye. "Had you kept up, maybe y'all would know who each other was dating. If anything, Ruth's a bystander in our family mess."

"You're right," he agreed, catching his clothes as I threw them his way. He dropped them into his duffle bag to take home. "But, you know what, it's de drama ah don't want any part of. Liam's my cousin...he's not some random guy." He zipped the bag. "If he still likes Ruth, ah can't be in de way. He knew her first...it's a matter of principles."

"You sure it's not a matter of pride?" I knew how men were about things like that. "Do you love her?"

Shadow sighed, sat on the edge of the bed, then looked at me with a smart-alec face. "Does a hog love slop?" That used to be his dad's answer for yes. I chuckled.

"Why Ruth, son-shine? What drew you to her?" He smiled, and that's what I wanted to see, his charming smile. All he needed was to remember his 'whys'.

Shadow removed his hat and scratched his hair. I knew those braids were coming out that night. "Besides you and Pa, Ruth's the greatest human I've ever met." His eyes grew moist. Any doubts I had were erased. "Ruthie Vega is kind, sensitive, thoughtful, loyal. Smart! She makes me laugh." He smiled wider. "Her faith is childlike and innocent. It's a joy to watch her. Ah can tell her anything, and..." He lowered his head as though thinking. "She gets me. Ah thought ah got her, too..." He stopped and put his face into his hands, frustrated. "But, maybe ah don't know her at all." He lifted his face and found my eyes for reassurance. "I'm just gonna be still and wait dis out."

"Being still and doing nothing are two different things." I wanted to coddle Shadow, but he was no longer my baby. He was a man who loved a woman and needed to acknowledge his abandonment anxieties. "There are three things that amaze me—no, four things that I don't understand...," I quoted one of my favorite verses as I walked toward the window, "...how an eagle glides through the sky, how a snake slithers on a rock, how a ship navigates the ocean, how a man loves a woman. It's all a mystery to me." I looked out the window. "But I do know one thing, TIME WAITS FOR NO ONE. Look, son," I pointed toward the driveway. "There goes your fair maiden." Ruth was leaving early. Bo sprung off the bed and was gone before I could tell him to catch her.

THIRTY-SIX

RUTH

The familiar faces hovering around dispersed and pretended to continue in their individual conversations. Luther Vandross was brought back full blast, crooning "Never Too Much."

I sighed, gazing beyond the man standing in front of me—causing drama and seeking attention, his usual modus operandi. He was no good for me. I turned to leave.

"Ruthie," Buggy called, grabbing my arm and quickly walking me to a semi-private corner on the deck. "I'm sorry." He half-heartedly apologized for all his drama. "It's just that it's good to see you." He smirked, offering me a seat.

"Nah," I responded, rolling my eyes, insisting on a quick conversation. "I'm straight." He chuckled.

"You can't be serious about all this farm crap?" His tall, broad body crowded my personal space. "Come on, we're cut from the same cloth. This ain't you." He took both of my hands and rocked them back and forth. "Our meeting again is fate."

"Are you serious?" I shook my head, snatching my hands from him. "Why are you doing this, Buggy? Why you gotta be so extra?" I could sense his mother, Mrs. Go, lurking and listening, so I lowered my elevated voice. "You don't even know who I am anymore."

Nothing I said phased him. Buggy bit down on his lip, massaging his goatee in a downward manner, ignoring everyone's feelings but his. "You know, ma-dukes told me that night you broke my heart that if we were meant to be, we'd find our way back to each other." He tried to take me into his arms, but I moved. "Ruthie, when I saw you walk through that door, I knew instantly that I had to have you back. Damn girl, you look good. Let Buggy take care of you." He had arms like an octopus; his hands were everywhere. I slapped them from around my waist.

"So, I'm supposed to believe that you want me back...and we're some sort of kindred spirits?" I asked sarcastically. He nodded, licking his lips and smiling. It irked me that I could now see how much he and Bo resembled. "Well, I don't think that chick you're with finds any of this amusing." A gaudy, artificial but attractive woman was staring at me with more attitude than Mrs. Go was giving. Buggy laughed.

"I'm Buggy, baby. Let's not get it twisted." He popped a fake collar. "I always have a chick on my arm." That was Buggy, non-committal to the very end. "But! There's only one you in my heart." He managed to get his lengthy arms around my waist again.

"Look, Buggy, I don't know what game you're playing, but please stop." I pulled them off. All I needed was for Bo to find him still all over me. "I don't love you like that anymore...and I know you don't have those feelings for me either. I AM, however, in love with your cousin." There, I had said it out loud. "I think he's the greatest person I've ever met."

Buggy sucked his teeth. "He's not in your league," he said in a patronizing tone.

I was getting mad. Buggy didn't know who I was. I wanted to curse him out, but I was trying to be civil and not ghetto amongst the crowd.

"Bo may not have experienced life as broadly as you, but he embraces it—deeply. His ability to absorb and understand life's balance is something you nor I may never get." I was poking my finger into his chest. "But, I tell you what...if you don't slow down, you'll find out the hard way about life." Ma Nay and her uncle, Pastor Josh, were being brought out. Bo wasn't with them. I sighed and turned my back. I didn't want Ma Nay to see me upset. "Since you're resurrecting the past, do you remember the guy I was with that day?" Buggy nodded and twisted his lips. "Well, I married him, and you may not wanna hear this, but y'all were just alike...all I did was jump out of the pot and into the flames."

"Pfft!" Buggy mouthed, shaking his head. "Never. That niguh won't nothing like me." The gun incident was still weld in his memory.

"Yeah, well, he was. He was arrogant and wanted the world by any means necessary, too. Just like you." I turned to make sure Ma Nay wasn't sneaking up on me. "Peewee was murdered." Buggy's face read, *yeah, when you play with guns, that's what happens.* "He lost his life running after the wrong things. I'm done with chasing dollars. That ain't me anymore." The image of Peewee and Junnie gunned down still haunted me, and I became slightly emotional. Buggy tried to retake my hand.

"Ruth—"

I moved from his reach. "You knew me as a little girl...I'm a grown woman now...and I've found a man who cares more about my soul than what's on the soles of my feet." I gestured with my hands, "Aren't you tired of bugging out yet, LIAM? I am..." God had allowed me to officially close that chapter. "You should slow down before the world turns on you too," I spoke of his drinking and the clown show he put on nightly for the media. I started to leave. Ma Nay looked confused. She was looking around for Bo, and I didn't know how to begin to explain what was happening. I needed some time alone. "I can't," I said, heading for the steps leading off the deck and into the yard. That voice inside, speaking against me, said, *What the hell are you doing here on a farm—a boricua from the Bronx?*

"I can't get you out of my system, girl!" Buggy yelled, belching out more foolishness and laughing.

"¡Vete pa'l carajo!" I responded, pissed. Hell seemed fitting for him.

THIRTY-SEVEN

BOAZ

"Ruth!" I yelled out, running toward her as fast as I could. She was getting in her car to leave. When she heard me, she stopped and waited, granting the encouragement I needed. "Ruth," I repeated, coming closer. The thought of this woman leaving me was overwhelming. I needed her more than I knew how to express. My whole heart was sewn in her web. I whispered to God, "Lord, keep me safe," intending on unguarding myself and facing the fears holding me captive. I didn't know what I would say, but I couldn't let Ruth leave.

I stopped running and continued toward her using cautious steps. She looked as though she'd been crying, and that broke me. I removed my hat and placed it over my heart.

"I'm a jerk," I said, ashamed of my thoughts and actions.

Ruth pounced from against the car, and with a puffy red face and an erect reprimanding finger swirling in the air she told me off. "If you're gonna be judging me...then maybe we should end this before it starts, because stacked-up my sins are hella' thick...and I do well enough on my own counting them."

She was even more beautiful when she was angry. I tucked my lips and bowed my head, trying not to chuckle. "I'm sorry." I really was. It had been so long since I'd dealt with a woman in that manner. The farm was my lady. "It's not you; it's me. I'm afraid of getting hurt. I'm afraid of losing...the people I love."

"Bo," she said in a softer perplexed tone, touching the hand with which I was anxiously wringing my hat. "Buggy and I ghosted each other years ago. I have no interest in him." I was glad to hear that but doubted my cousin felt the same. If Liam had feelings for Ruth, he'd make our lives a living hell trying to get her back, and I cared for drama about as much as I cared for toothaches. I placed my hat back on my head and took Ruth's hands, staring her straight in the eyes.

"Ruth, my feelings for you haven't changed." She started to tear up again. "Ahh, man." I lowered and shook my head, frustrated with myself. I hated to see a woman cry—especially over something I did. "Look, I'm not trying to get my heart broken or break yours either. I'm just trying to live de best life ah can and take care of my mama...no drama," I declared, highlighting the latter part. "I've had enough heartache...and truth be told, lak ah said, I'm afraid of losing people—maybe so much so dat ah hide...and ah know dat's wrong." I released her hands and folded my arms across my chest. I was ashamed. "Ah cut a lot of people off, sheltering my emotions. Liam is one of 'em...but he's still my cousin...and ah absolutely need to know dat he's over you."

Ruth shook her head and frowned. "Yeah," she declared in absolute assurance. "The only person Buggy loves is Buggy...he's just drunk and upset that you have something that was his."

I definitely understood how Liam might have felt that way. It irked me thinking of him and Peewee being with her. Ruth had a past that I couldn't erase. Despite it, I wanted her to be my future.

Ruth unfolded my arms and took my hands, this time smiling. "Listen, in your own words—Mr. Bo, that's lipstick on a pig. It's a done deal." I smiled. Those were my father's words. "To be honest. I don't care how Buggy feels."

Ruth was right. She and I belonged to each other. I pulled her into an embrace, and squeezed her tightly. I was in my head too much. Buggy's feelings weren't valid.

Throw off everything that hinders. Run the race that's marked for you, I told myself.

"Ah think I've been so busy trying to live up to Pa's legacy dat ah failed him." I realized out loud, resting my cheek against Ruth's thick black locks. They smelled of something sweet. "I've been foolish...pigheaded, and scared to love. Ma was right, ah put my heart up on a shelf instead of trusting God's will for it." I pressed my lips down on Ruth's head and kissed her. "Forgive me...because ah love you with every fiber of my being and ah won't rest until ah fix dis Liam thing."

Ruth looked up at me. We both had tears in our eyes. Mine felt like chains falling off. I felt winded but free from restraining myself from her.

"Then we need to hurry up and fix it." She could barely speak. "Because I love you too." We both sort of laughed at ourselves, then confirmed our pledge of love with a kiss so deep that it warmed my spirit.

As they say, when love comes you just know. Everything is right with the world. I knew from the moment I saw Ruth that there was something about her. She ignited a fire in me that had been put out. She says that I redeemed her but what happened is that she lifted me.

· · ·

Wɪᴛʜ ᴍʏ ꜰᴀᴍɪʟʏ spread around me enjoying the festivities, I sat with Ruth by my side at a patio set on the deck. I called my cousin using a corporate tone, "Liam! Can you come o'va here and sit down for a sec, please. Ah wanna talk to you."

Liam came, taking long confident strides across the floor, coyly smiling and enjoying a crawfish etouffee stuffed baked potato dish Ma made. Ruth squeezed my hand tightly. We promised that we would talk it through no matter what he said. So, we sat down together.

Liam leaned over his plate, sort of flexing his jaw muscle. "What's up, cuz," he said like nothing happened. Ruth was right. He was a gaslighter. An instigator. "Mmm. Yo, Tante Rah!" He yelled toward Ma after shoveling a spoon of food into his mouth. "This baked potato is slappin'! Those fancy restaurants in LA don't got nothing on you." Ma smiled, taking a bow.

"Liam," I interrupted, this time squinting my eyes and clenching my own jaw muscles. I was trying to remain calm.

"You need to franchise...I'd invest," he continued ignoring me.

"Buggy," Ruth repeated, frustrated herself.

"Word, this is crazy good," he whispered, licking his fingers before looking up at us. "I'm here," he answered sarcastically, when he was good and ready. There was an apparent disconnect between us, despite his drinking. I knew about it but it didn't bother or affect me until that moment.

"Listen, whatever happened between us, I'm sorry." I decided to apologize instead of being angry with him. Liam was hurting, and we used to be so close.

He looked me in the eyes and continued chewing. Then, he placed his fork on his plate and wiped his mouth. "I'm the mickey-fickey man. I'm like the Black Jesus out here." He responded with an air of arrogance. "You think I'm stressed over ya-azz." He laughed cold-heartedly. "Baby, come here." He called for the woman he had brought with him. "I'm good, cuz," he said as he wrapped his arm around her exaggerated hips. Do I look like I'll be losing sleep over this?" High is how he looked, inflamed with alcohol. I became even more concerned. "Baby, try this." He attempted to feed the woman.

"I had some, Buggy," she insisted, trying to keep him from shoving the spoon into her mouth. "It's delicious. I told you to try it, remember?"

"Taste it!" He demanded, force-feeding her.

"Listen...," I couldn't take it anymore. I had to leave. I wasn't going to get into a fight with my cousin over the treatment of a woman I didn't know. "Ah just wanted to tell you dat ah love you and I'm sorry... 'bout er'rything." I stood to leave, taking Ruth's hand. Trying to have a conversation with Liam was a waste. He was putting on a show as he did on television. His reality was confused. "I miss how we used to chill, that's all," I added, and Liam stood with me. We were equally tall and fit in stature. Standing there eye to eye, I could see a glimpse of my favorite cousin peeking through his blank gaze. But if he wanted Ruth, he would have to fight me for her.

"Liam," I said, gripping firmly the fist he put up for a pound. "Ruth is my lady, and ah ain't letting her go. Ah hope dat doesn't put any more strain on our relationship." Ruth placed her hand on my back, reminding me that she was there as support. I turned toward her. She was still that vision in white. "Ah love her," I added, mostly speaking to Ruth, then released Liam's hand and took hers. *I love her.* The words resonated in my spirit and life suddenly felt too short to take for granted. "As a matter of fact." I got down on one knee. *What am I waiting for?* The music stopped, and the oohs and ahhs of those eavesdropping could be heard.

With my family as witnesses, I looked up into the eyes of the woman I love and asked, "Ruth, will you marry me? Ah promise to love and care for you every day of my life." Ma ran over and yanked Pa's ring off her finger, handing it to me.

Ruth squealed in utter delight. "Yes!" She looked to her mother-in-law for approval. Cousin Nay nodded and started a chain of claps.

"We are witnesses!" All those surrounding us chanted.

I placed the ring that fit perfectly on Ruth's finger and kissed her hand. Surprisingly, Liam extended his hand to help me up. We hugged it out briefly before I received my bride-to-be into my arms.

"I guess I just want my friend back, too." Liam half smiled with his arms folded defensively. "I'm sorry...you know I'm always bugging out," he added, before spreading his arms with an equally wide grin. The responsibility to love and commit to Ruth suddenly became a burden he didn't want to take on.

"We good, cuz," I said, engaging him in a handshake. There was no need to squander energy on uselessness.

"You got a good woman, Shadow. Best on the block." He gave Ruth a sideways hug. "We cool?"

"Yeah," she smiled, giving Liam a full embrace.

Paw-Paw was led over, and he wrapped his arms around Ruth and me.

"Besides opening my eyes dis morning," he faintly said, teary-eyed. "Y'all have given me de best birthday gift today." He pulled us in closer, forming a circle around him before giving his blessing. "May de Lord make dis woman who is coming into your home, Shadow, lak Rachel and Leah. May she have lots of chil'ren runnin' through de halls. Ah may not live to see it, but ah pray dat you and your family prosper in all you do." I bowed so Paw-Paw could kiss my cheek, then Ruth's.

"Come on, let's party!" Liam yelled, interrupting the moment. "I got a few mo' hours in this weed-infested desert with you peasants before I'm Audi 5000. Let's do this! Jay-Skii," he yelled toward Mama's friend, the DJ, "Se-lec-tah," he added in his father's native tongue. "Play dat Maze jam!" He shook up a bottle of champagne that his lady friend handed him, popped it open, and sprayed it in the air as "Before I Let Go" played.

"Woo-hoo!" We yelled and partied into the night, even after Paw-Paw was driven home.

THIRTY-EIGHT

NAOMI

So Boaz took Ruth into his home, and she became his wife. When he slept with her, the Lord enabled her to become pregnant—something He hadn't done for my Peewee. Ruth gave birth to a son.

The women of Delery Street said to me, "Praise God, who has now provided a redeemer for your family! May this child be prosperous. May he restore your youth and care for you in your old age. For he is the son of your daughter-in-law who loves you and has been better to you than seven sons!"

I took the baby, cuddled him to my breast, and cared for him as if he were my own.

The neighborhood women said, "Now, at last, Naomi has a son again!"

Bo and Ruth named the baby Obed Joshua Abrams. Obed means, 'a servant of God'. A worshiper. We call him Bear because he was a whopping ten pounds, eleven ounces, and twenty-two inches long at birth. Bear loves his Nana, and Nana loves him.

The kids and I moved into the mini-mansion. Unfortunately, my dear friend Gladys died of cancer. One day she was on chemo; the next, she was gone. The poor thing held it secret because she only wanted my companionship, not pity. Because of Gladys, I was given back pieces from the past—nothing that could replace those lost—we can never get back what is lost, but fond memories through pictures that I thought were destroyed by Katrina.

Gladys loved pictures, and she had tons of them. She had taken her albums when we fled from our homes. They were full of memories of the twins growing up with her kids—Jackie and Ben. Pictures of us together with Eli enjoying life and companionship on Delery Street. I treasure the memories, as I do her. Gladys will forever be in my heart.

Along with time comes healing and new memories. Rah married her DJ friend, Jayson. They travel the country when she's not cooking at the Café and loving on our grandbaby, Bear. Buggy was right about her franchising. Ms. Pie's pies hit the markets hard! Especially after she won that cooking competition on television. She allowed Ruth the opportunity to utilize her degrees, giving her full authority over her brand.

It's funny, I came back to NOLA with nothing. Little did I know, I came back with everything. God builds the hearts of the people he's going to place together. Sometimes His grace doesn't look like how we imagine. Sometimes we have to endure through pain, struggle, and loss. Hang in there, God's plan remains perfect. There's an old adage that says. If you're going to pray, why worry, and if you're going to worry, why pray? Our problems pale when we view them in the light of His Presence. Through everything, God is at work.

. . .

LORD, we thank you. You have blessed us abundantly in so many ways. My ears have heard you, but now my eyes have seen you, too. Katrina wasn't the best thing that's ever happened to me, but it forced me out of my comfort zone. Praise the name of the Lord forever.

THE END

EPILOGUE

THE BOOK OF RUTH

It was made clear from the beginning of the book of Ruth that Ruth was a Moabite woman. But who were the Moabites?

In Genesis, we are told many stories of family betrayal, lust, escape, scandal, and incest. In one particular story, a man named Lot, a relative of Abraham living in the pagan district of Sodom, hospitably asks two visitors to stay the night at his home. Now, it just so happens that these two visitors are angels disguised as men.

Sometime during this extraordinary visitation, the community catches wind of the new guests in town. The men of Sodom, both old and young, gathered around Lot's home, demanding that he hand his guests over so that they may 'have their way' with them (hence the word sodomy gets its root). Of course, Lot is appalled and admonishes them for their wickedness. Still he offers the mob his two virgin daughters. Perhaps, from his perspective, this was the slightly lesser of two terrible evils. When the assembly refuses Lot's offer, the angels take the lead, striking them all with blindness. Amid the confusion, they warn Lot to take his family and flee the city—for it will be destroyed by the wrath of God.

Lot and his daughters find shelter in Zoar; from there to a cave in the mountains. According to Jewish tradition, Lot's daughters believed that the entire world had been destroyed and they were the only survivors. So, they resorted to incest to preserve the human race. The Bible says that the firstborn said, *'We may preserve the seed of our father'.* Lot's eldest daughter then gets him drunk and has sex with him—*and he did not know when she laid down or arose.* The following night, the younger daughter does the same. They both become pregnant. The older daughter gives birth to Moab. Guess who is a descendent of Moab (the father of the Moabites, born of incest, Pagans)? Ruth.

Ruth is one of the most significant Moabite figures in the bible, and is one of the few Moabites mentioned as having a genealogical connection with Jesus. In Ruth's story, we find a woman cursed by heritage yet, through her marriage, is intermingled with the hope of a chosen people. Ruth was not part of the covenant people of God. Despite this, it is through her that God's covenant promise is furthered when she marries a kinsman redeemer, Boaz. In the Jewish custom, a redeemer is a person who, as the nearest relative, is charged with the duty of restoring the rights and avenging his relative's wrongs. According to Naomi, Boaz was her husband's redeemer.

When Naomi's husband and sons die, she is left alone with two foreign daughters-in-law in a pagan land. Through Naomi's wisdom, she abandons the land where her deceased husband brought her and ventures back home with her new companions. Before this trek begins, Naomi loses a daughter-in-law who decides to return to her culture, her people, and their beloved god of Chemosh. Her daughter-in-law, Ruth, remains, pledging her loyalty to Naomi and God.

Though in the beginning, Naomi felt bitter about her predicament and loss, her faith was still alive. She trusted God and became the voice of wisdom spoken throughout the book of Ruth. Back in Bethlehem it is through Naomi's kindness and love that Ruth meets the God of her mother-in-law's faith and also becomes a faithful believer and living testimony to Him.

Although the book of Ruth is titled after one woman, it is obviously about three individuals placed together for a specific time and purpose. If Naomi was responsible for Ruth's inward change then Boaz confirmed the change and was rewarded to them both for their faithfulness.

Boaz, the son of Rahab (the Canaanite harlot) and Salmon (an Israelite hero) was a wealthy landowner and relative to Elimelech, Naomi's husband. He notices Ruth working in his fields and goes far and beyond to show her favor. Ruth witnessed from the beginning how godly and kind Boaz was. She saw his love for the Lord, his obedience to God's law, his respect toward women, his empathy for the poor, and his generosity.

The story of Ruth illustrates God's ability to inspire people to have faith in Him through average day-to-day activities. All the characters in the Book of Ruth face life's normal challenges and discover God is weaving a story of redemption out of all the details. The book also depicts His grace in showing forgiveness, as he did with Lot. God chooses 'the foolish and the weak' to bless His people and establish His promises. Ruth is a prime example of this. She may not have always recognized God's guidance, yet she came to know Him through the people placed in her life. Her gleaning in the fields of her deceased husband's close relative was more than a coincidence. Ruth ended up marrying Boaz and instead of working the fields, she owned them.

Ruth and Boaz had a son named Obed. Obed had Jesse and Jesse had King David. From the prostitute Rahab and the Moabite Ruth came the lineage of Jesus Christ. One choice, the choice to believe, changed the trajectory of their lives. The people in the Book of Ruth are a classic example of the godly at their best—imitating God's faithfulness through loving and loyal relationships. **God bless.**

CHARACTER GLOSSARY

Ruth - After being widowed, Ruth remains with her mother-in-law. Ruth is the great-grandmother of King David, and mentioned in the genealogy of Christ.
   Ruth, Gospel of Matthew

Salmon - Married to Rahab. Father of Boaz. Great-great-grandfather of King David.
   1 Chronicles, Ruth, Matthew, and Luke

Naomi - Ruth's mother-in-law. Naomi's life illustrates the power of God to bring something good out of bitter circumstances.
   Ruth

Boaz - The son of Salmon and Rahab. He was a wealthy man from Bethlehem, the great grand-father of King David, and also mentioned in the genealogy of Christ.
   Ruth, Gospel of Matthew

Elimelech - Naomi's husband. He was of the tribe of Judah and lived in Bethlehem.
Ruth

Mahlon - Son of Elimelech and Naomi. First husband of Ruth.
Ruth

Kilion - Son of Elimelech and Naomi. Husband of Orpah.
Ruth

Joshua - One of the twelve spies of Israel sent by Moses to explore the land of Canaan. Joshua led the Israelite tribes in the conquest of Canaan.
Joshua, Deuteronomy, Numbers

Rahab - A harlot in Jericho. Believed in the Lord. Hid the Hebrew spies and was saved when the walls of Jericho came tumbling down. Great-great-grandmother of King David.
Joshua, Matthew, Hebrews, James

Orpah - The Moabite woman married to Kilion who decided to stay with her people when her husband died.
Ruth

DISCUSSION QUESTIONS & BIBLE STUDY

Read Ruth Chapter One or Part One

1. What motivated biblical Ruth to stay with Naomi instead of returning to Moab?
2. What motivated fictional Ruth to stay with Naomi instead of returning to New York City?
3. What does worshiping other gods look like today? What things did the characters in the book worship?
4. *Read Hebrews 13:15:16* - What sacrifice does God want from us? What sacrifices did both biblical and fictional Ruth make?

Read Ruth Chapter Two or Part Two

1. What type of man was Boaz?
2. How can we implement the characteristics of Boaz into our daily lives, marriages, businesses/work?

3. What was it about both biblical and fictional Ruth that impressed Boaz?
4. Do you believe in love at first sight? Was it love at first sight?

Read Ruth Chapter Three or Part Three

1. Was the biblical and fictional Naomi's advice helpful to Ruth?
2. Did she plot for Boaz's affection?
3. How did both biblical and fictional Boaz respond to Ruth's actions?
4. Why didn't Boaz make the first move? What did he think of himself?
5. What postponed Boaz from committing to Ruth? What did he promise?
6. Why did he first kinsman decide not to redeem Ruth?

Read Ruth Chapter Four or Part Three

1. Naomi receives Boaz and Ruth's son Obed as her grandson. In what ways did Obed become Naomi's redeemer?
2. *Read Matthew 1:5-6* - What are Boaz, Ruth and Obed now famous for?
3. *Read Galatians 4:4-5 and 1 Peter 1:18-19* - Who is our redeemer, and what sacrifice did He make to redeem us?

Questions from the author

1. Did this book help with your understanding of the biblical book of Ruth?
2. Is this your first time reading a book by JC Miller?
3. Would you recommend this book to others? If so, please leave a review on Amazon and share your experience on social media.
4. I love to hear from readers. Let me know how you feel about this book, and what other biblical characters would you like to read about? Email JC Miller at askjcmiller@gmail.com.

FINDING
GOD
in the
KITCHEN
Ms. Pie's Recipes

JC MILLER

LETTER TO THE READER

Dear Reader:

Surprise! Here are a few recipes developed from the fictional dishes created in JC Miller's novel, *Something About Ruth*. In the book, one of the characters, lovingly called Ms. Pie—originally Rahab from Miller's trilogy, *I Am Rahab: A Novel* (based on the life of the biblical harlot). Ms. Pie is a chef, mother, widow, and entrepreneur who creates farm-to-table fresh dishes that are regarded as culinary masterpieces.

With these recipes, Jess, Mo' Books hopes to forge intimate moments made over food for our readers. As Ms. Pie narrates through some of her favorite childhood recipes, use them to commune with family and friends. Bring a dish and share the love. Let us know how they turn out: **Askjcmiller@gmail.com**

Bon Appetit

JC Miller

Jess, Mo' Books

L&L SUGAH

There is something special about the pairing of lemon and lavender. The combination is like sunshine and summertime. Whenever Big Mama made it, the aroma filled the house. I knew it would find its way into a bit of everything. This infused sugar is amazing! It will turn a regular day into a special moment. Big Mama put out a jar of Lemon & Lavender (L&L Sugah) every Thanksgiving or whenever she baked. She probably would have made it more often, but because lemon zest oils dissipate quickly, it had to be used promptly. At the restaurant, we put it out regularly, and it goes FAST! The customers love it.

INGREDIENTS

- 1 cup of organic cane sugar
- 1 lemon, preferably organic
- 2 teaspoons of dried lavender buds (we grow ours, but they are sold on Amazon in bulk)

INSTRUCTIONS

1. Wash and dry the lemon. Using a peeler, carefully remove the zest from the entire lemon. (Make sure to remove only the yellow part, not the bitter white part underneath). Save the peeled lemon for our cookie recipe or lemonade.
2. Put ½ cup cane sugar plus lavender buds and lemon zest into a food processor. Pulse to combine. Then blend until L&L is fully incorporated into the sugar. (This will take a minute or so. Make sure that there are no big lemon pieces left behind. It is okay if you see some lavender buds. But you want fine zest).
3. Take a look...and don't forget this step—inhale. This sugar is so fragrant. I smile every time. (It should look moist and beautiful).
4. Add the other ½ cup of cane sugar and blend again. (If you see chunks of zest, process a little longer).

Voila!! You now have lemon and lavender-infused sugar.

Some suggested uses for L&L Sugah:

- Sweeten your tea (it's amazing) or coffee if you're daring. No cream.
- Stir it into lemonade.
- Sprinkle it on top of fresh fruit.
- Add it to homemade whipped cream.
- Mix it into muffin, cookie, pancake, or waffle batter.

Note:

- Use L&L Sugah in your baking recipes immediately for the freshest results.
- Make and use the proper amount of sugar your recipes call for.
- Always use the zest of one lemon per cup of sugar. (The lavender bud amount can be adjusted to taste).
- Store the L&L Sugah in a glass jar or a zip-lock bag in the refrigerator. (Remember to use it before the end of the day as the oils in lemon zest dissipate quickly).
- You can also make lavender sugar on its own. It holds up well. Use the same recipe above, omitting the lemon. If you let it sit for a day or two, the lavender flavor will develop more.

Why lemon and lavender?

Both lemon and lavender have healing properties that help relax and energize you at the same time.

Benefits of lavender: Treatment for anxiety, depression, intestinal problems, insomnia, restlessness, and pain.

Benefits of lemon:

- It can be calming and stimulating.
- It has a long list of powerful properties, including: astringent, antiseptic, antifungal, and more.

L&L HEMP COOKIES

Big Mama was an herbalist. It is safe to say that she made these cookies weekly for her clients dealing with anxiety and depression. Big Mama used homemade cannabis butter. At the restaurant, we make our cookies kid-friendly using hemp oil. For special customers, we will use a CBD tincture. These cookies are another great way to enjoy the refreshing flavors of lemon and lavender! The addition of hemp oil is a bonus.

For the best results, this recipe is made with fresh organic ingredients, but organic is not required. Big Mama raised chickens, and she always had an ol' cow in the yard. Organic foods were readily available to us.

Note: Hemp seeds and dried lavender are edible and medicinal herbs.

INGREDIENTS

- 1 stick of butter plus 8 tablespoons of butter, softened

- ¾ cup L&L Sugah
- 1 egg yolk at room temperature
- 2 tablespoons of freshly squeezed lemon juice
- 1 ½ cups unbleached cake flour
- ½ cup arrowroot powder (or cornstarch)
- Pinch of pink Himalayan salt
- (optional) ½ teaspoon or 1 teaspoon of hemp oil. (Omitting will not change the taste).

INSTRUCTIONS

1. Cream the butter and sugar together for 5 minutes with a stand mixer or hand mixer. Big Mama used her own muscles!
2. When well combined, add hemp oil.
3. Add the egg yolk and lemon juice and stir to combine.
4. Add the flour, arrowroot powder, and salt. Stir everything together until the cookie dough begins to hold up.
5. Take the cookie dough out of the bowl and form it into a log.
6. Wrap the dough log in parchment paper, wax paper, or plastic wrap. Fold ends under or twist to close.
7. Refrigerate the dough log for 20 minutes or until firm.
8. When ready to cook, preheat the oven to 310°F and slice the chilled log into ¼-inch rounds.
9. Place the rounds on a parchment-lined baking sheet about an inch apart.
10. Bake for about 20-25 minutes. (Check closely after 20 minutes, as cookies will start to brown quickly). Take the cookies out when only the edges are barely golden. The centers will still be fairly soft.

11. Let the cookies cool on the baking sheet for several minutes before transferring them to a cooling rack. They will firm up as they cool (it will be hard to resist tasting one, but I promise you they taste better completely cooled!).

These cookies taste like summertime! Buttery, lemony, herbaceous, and slightly sweet. The lavender flavor really shines through! What's best is the cookies are not loaded with ingredients that are horrible for you, so feel free to treat yourself to a few!

Notes:

- Recipe makes 20 to 24 cookies
- You can store the dough log for several days in the fridge (for several weeks in the freezer).
- Hemp seeds are from a species of Cannabis sativa *but are not the same as marijuana.*
- The oil derived from hemp seeds contain less than 0.5% of THC, a psychoactive compound.

Benefits of hemp seed:

- It is an excellent source of essential daily dietary nutrients and safe for adults and kids.
- On their own, hemp seeds don't have much flavor. Which makes them a perfect blend for smoothies and other foods.
- Hemp oil is an easy way to boost nutrition.

SWEET PUPPIES

Hush puppies or hoe cakes are a southern side dish staple. Growing up, Big Mama made them in a big black cast iron pan filled with o'l, as she would say. She'd serve-em-up hot with fried fish on Fridays, beans and greens on Sundays, and other days with a hot gumbo. When we had leftovers, I ate them as an after-school snack—hot, with the cinnamon honey butter Big Mama kept in the fridge.

Big Mama always had a little garden growing. She was into organic and holistic living before it was a thing. So, while hush puppies are a staple southern side dish, adding sweet potatoes was a Big Mama thang. And babee! It is so worth it.

INGREDIENTS

- 4 cups vegetable or canola oil
- 2 medium sweet potatoes, peeled, cooked, and mashed. (about 1½ cups).
- ¼ cup local buttermilk

- 1 egg
- 1 tablespoon brown sugar
- 1 cup white or yellow stone cornmeal
- ½ cup unbleached self-rising flour (We use King Arthur's)
- 1 teaspoon Himalayan salt
- 1 fresh scallion, chopped
- 2-4 slices of bacon cooked and crumbled.
- (optional) ½ of jalapeno pepper or ½ red bell pepper thinly diced. No seeds. (It is not spicy. It lends a nice taste).
- (optional) ½ teaspoon cayenne pepper. (Why not kick it up a notch?)

INSTRUCTIONS

1. Poke holes into 2 medium-sized sweet potatoes with a fork. Wrap them in foil, place them on a baking sheet, and bake in a 400-degree oven until soft. (This step is optional. You can peel and boil 'em, or nuke 'em in the microwave if time is an issue). Big Mama would always bake them so that they cooked in their own sweet juices. The same for her sweet potato pies.
2. Make the Cinna' Butta while your potatoes are baking. (See next recipe). Let it chill in the fridge until ready to serve.
3. Fry you some bacon. Crumble and set aside. Save the grease for the field pea recipe.
4. Heat vegetable or canola oil in a large dutch oven or deep fryer over medium-high heat to 350°F.

5. While waiting for oil to come to temperature, place mashed sweet potatoes, buttermilk, egg, and brown sugar in a large bowl and whisk to combine.

6. Add cornmeal, flour, salt, cayenne, bacon, scallion, and peppers to the bowl. Stir to combine. (Do not over mix).

7. Once the oil has reached 350°F, carefully place the hush puppy batter into the oil using a greased standard ice cream scoop or a tablespoon. (Do not overcrowd).

8. Fry the hush puppies for about 3 minutes, turning them occasionally until browned. If you're using a deep fryer--once they float to the top they're pretty much done. (If the oil is too hot, the cookies will brown quickly and be undercooked inside). Test one for doneness.

9. Using a slotted spoon, remove the hush puppies from the oil and set them aside to drain on a wire rack or paper towel. (Place in the oven on a warm setting to keep them hot while you fry the next batch).

Notes:

- Makes 16 to 18 hush puppies.
- Serve with Cinna' Butta or Uptown Syrup Butta. Recipes on the following pages.

Benefits of sweet potatoes:

- Plenty of antioxidant qualities.
- High in fiber.

CINNA' BUTTA

This was essential in our house. Big Mama had a sweet tooth. She put cinnamon honey butter in our hot oats, on toast, and, on Sundays, she'd spread it on biscuits with a side of scrambled eggs and bacon or sausage. Try it! It does not disappoint.

INGREDIENTS

- 1 stick unsalted butter, softened
- ¼ cup powdered sugar
- 1 tablespoon raw honey
- ½ teaspoon pure vanilla extract
- 1½ teaspoons ground cinnamon
- ⅛ teaspoon Himalayan sea salt

INSTRUCTIONS

1. Add all the ingredients to a bowl.

2. Mix with a standing or hand mixer. Beat until well combined and fluffy.
3. Serve at room temperature on your favorite bread or breakfast food.

Note:

- Store in an airtight container in the refrigerator for up to one month.
- You can leave it out at room temperature during cool months for up to 1 week.
- Use Cinna' Butta to replace the butter and sugar in your cornbread batter.

UPTOWN SYRUP BUTTA

Okay, I created this recipe while living with my mother in the Bronx. Big Mama loved her sweets, however, her daughter (my mother, Poo) loved heat! She was that person who put hot sauce on popcorn; that is until I put her on to this delicious spicy maple syrup butter. Changed her life!

INGREDIENTS

- 1 stick unsalted butter, softened
- 3 tablespoons pure maple syrup
- 1½ teaspoons hot-pepper sauce, or to your taste. (Use your favorite brand. We make ours with fresh garden ingredients.)
- ½ teaspoon coarse Himalayan salt

INSTRUCTIONS

1. Mash together all ingredients in a bowl with a spatula until smooth.

Note:

- Uptown Syrup Butta can be stored in the refrigerator up to 3 days. Bring to room temperature before serving.
- To turn this recipe into syrup for chicken and waffles, according to your taste, increase the maple syrup, decrease the butter, and the hot-pepper sauce stays the same. Warm everything in a small pot on low until melted together.

PINK EYED PEAS

I'm especially fond of the purple hull pea. Big Mama and I used to shuck baskets full of them while sitting on the porch sipping sweet tea and listening to old zydeco records. We would make a day of it, because, eventually, Ms. Ruby and the First Lady would come by with even more baskets full.

When purple hull peas are in season, we stock up by fresh freezing them to use throughout the year. When we start running low, we mix them with snap beans and okra to stretch it out until the next season.

INGREDIENTS

- Bacon grease (we always have some saved, but if you don't, render out the fat of a couple of slices of bacon).
- 1 medium country ham hock
- 1½ - 2 pounds fresh or frozen purple hull peas
- 32 ounces sodium-free chicken broth
- 1 Maggi chicken bouillon cube

- 2 cups water, more or less as needed to cover the peas
- ½ teaspoon seasoning salt
- ½ teaspoon onion powder
- 1 teaspoon fresh ground pepper, we like McCormick
- Scallions for garnish
- Cooked white rice or cornbread

INSTRUCTIONS

1. Parboil ham hock in 2 cups of water in a dutch oven over medium heat for an hour, giving it time to soften and burst open.
2. Break up the meat and add the peas and bacon fat to the pot.
3. Slowly add the chicken broth and crumble a Maggi cube over the peas. Add more water if needed. The liquid should slightly cover the peas.
4. Loosely cover the pot and bring it to a boil, then reduce to a simmer.
5. Cook for another hour.
6. Taste the broth and add salt if needed.
7. Add ground pepper and onion powder to taste.
8. Press a pea against the side of the pot. Peas should be tender but not mushy when done.
9. Garnish with chopped scallion.

Serve over white rice or as the star with a side of Sweet Puppies.

Notes:

- Fresh and frozen peas cook much faster than dried beans and don't require any soaking.

- Southern Purple Hull Peas or Pink Eyes are a variety of field pea.
- While similar, each one adds its own quality.
- Black Eyed peas are the most popular or commonly used field pea.

Purple Hull Peas vs Black Eyed Peas

Purple hull (pink eyed) peas and black eyed peas look very much alike. However, there is a noticeable pinkness to the eye of the purple hull pea. Black eyed peas are described as having a more earthy taste.

JUST LAK DAT SWEET TEA

Sweet tea is a go-to southern drink. I love to jazz mine up with fruit. This pineapple sweet tea is so refreshing. It hits the spot on a hot summer day! Big Mama used to start hers with sun-brewed tea then she kicked it up a notch. Ahhh!

INGREDIENTS

- One 20-ounce can of pineapple chunks
- 4 family-size or 6 regular black tea bags (your favorite brand)
- 2 cups boiling water plus 9 additional cups of cold
- 1 cup sugar
- A teeny pinch of baking soda

INSTRUCTIONS

1. Boil 2 cups of water.

2. Pour over tea bags into a heat-safe measuring cup or pot. Sprinkle in a pinch of baking soda and let the tea steep for 5 minutes.

3. Remove the tea bags and add sugar. Stir until dissolved.

4. Into a large gallon jug or pitcher, add the pineapples (including the juice) plus 1 cup of water. Stir to mix slightly. (If you're using a spouted container, you may want to eliminate the pineapple chunks as they may clog. Try freezing them in ice cubes instead).

5. Pour the hot tea and sugar mixture into the pitcher over the pineapples.

6. Stir, making sure the sugar is dissolved. Finally, add 8 cups of cold water to the pitcher and refrigerate until serving.

When ready to serve, fill your cup with ice before pouring the sweet tea over it. Garnish with a mint leaf or add a teaspoon of L&L Sugah. Enjoy!

Tip: Baking soda *neutralizes the tannins in black tea, giving it a smoother taste.* This same trick takes the bitterness out of green tea. You can add a small pinch to a mug of hot tea as it steeps.

Enjoy!

Join us on Facebook at Finding God in the
Kitchen Group to see our pictures...and
please share yours!

Because sharing is caring, here's another added bonus!

Use the QR codes below to enjoy handpicked playlists created especially for this book on Spotify.

Ruth: Bounce Playlist

RUTH: Rebirth Playlist

Also by the Author

For more fun recipes, get JC Miller's devotional cookbook, Finding God in the Kitchen, Christ and Cake.

Other inspirational titles by JC Miller are available now on Amazon!

JC's Amazon Page

ABOUT THE AUTHOR

JC Miller is a freshly anointed, faith-based author who uses her childhood experiences in the Bronx, New York, to capture the soul of inner-city living. As a former student of Chicago's Moody Bible Institute and a graduate of the Te'Hillah School of Urban Ministry, Miller utilizes her studies to intertwine pop culture with divine accounts of biblical characters. Through sharing these stories, her goals are to encourage people to study the bible and not make it complicated, to view themselves through the lives of those characterized, and to find healing in Christ.

JC Miller recently co-founded a publishing company, Jess, Mo' Books, with her childhood friend, M.R. Spain. Together, these ladies are creating fresh content to uplift, educate, and motivate women through blogs, social media groups, and a yearly online magazine.